SEEING

STRANGERS

SEEING

STRANGERS

SEBASTIAN J. PLATA

The following is a work of fiction. Names, characters, places, events and incidents are either the product of the author's imagination or used in an entirely fictitious manner. Any resemblance to actual persons, living or dead, is entirely coincidental.

ISBN 978-1-951709-79-2
eISBN: 978-1-951709-98-3

Library of Congress Control Number: available upon request

First hardcover edition July 2022 by Agora Books
An imprint of Polis Books, LLC
44 Brookview Lane
Aberdeen, NJ 07747
www.PolisBooks.com

For Mitsu

CHAPTER 1

One of the main reasons hookup apps are so damn addictive has to do with their utter unpredictability. You can log into Grindr every ten minutes all day at work and get nothing but crickets. And then you can be on the train home, exhausted because you had to work much later than usual, waiting for the team in Shenzhen to approve your translation of an online campaign, and you open Grindr one last time and boom—a message from a hot, muscly Latino, asking if you want to come over.

Just as the train doors are about to slide shut, I jump up from my seat and dash onto the platform. This is the right thing to do in this type of situation. Grindr is a location-based app and you don't want to put any unnecessary distance between yourself and your heaven-sent hunk.

Heart hammering, I sit on an empty platform bench while the train and commuter foot traffic leave me entirely alone with the rats.

Hey, I type. *I'm down. Where are you?*

While I wait for an answer, I take a good look at the guy's profile. It has no public photo and, in its description, only says:

6'4", masc, discreet. As it's not very informative, I go back to reexamine the photos he's sent me directly.

The guy is one hundred percent my type. Tall, dark, handsome. I'm a sucker for conventionally attractive dudes and this one looks like he was plucked right out of a car commercial in which he played the sexy young father of a two-year-old.

The photo of him with his arm around a blonde girl's shoulders—both of them wearing sunglasses in some Southwestern desert setting—is a great showcase for his height and his fit, proportional body, which he shows off in nothing but boxer briefs in another very enticing mirror selfie. He's muscular but not too muscular, more athletic than gym-sculpted, and has a good amount of chest hair. In the waist-up photo taken on some kind of forest hike, even though, again, he's got sunglasses on, you can see his thick neck and symmetrical smile. And the cock pic? Holy shit the cock pic. Speaking of symmetrical. If I were as talented as my artist husband Cristian and someone asked me to draw the perfect penis, this is what I'd come up with.

I feel a flicker of "too good to be true", the way I sometimes do when really hot guys hit me up. The person who sent me the photos could, of course, be deceiving me. He might resemble the man in them to a degree but be a totally different person altogether, and, chances are, a much less attractive one. But, then again, this is New York, home to the cream of the crop in all categories, including physical appearance. So, chances that he's in fact real are just as high. You just never know.

A message containing nothing else but an address pops up on my screen and my pulse quickens. Usually, when you receive a specific address, the guy means serious business. I copy it into Google maps, which informs me that it's a fourteen minute walk from where I am currently, the Jefferson Ave L train stop.

Since Mr. Heaven-Sent is wearing sunglasses in all his photos, my normal procedure would be to request a pic where you can see his face clearly without them, but that type of demand, no matter how reasonable, could potentially turn him off. I know from experience how impatient people on these apps can be. Especially hot ones who are on the down-low. My gut is telling me to go with it before he changes his mind, and before things become less convenient for me.

Be there in ten, I reply and stand up.

Cristian already knows I'm working late so I don't even bother letting him know. This tiny detour won't make much of a difference and I'm already so close to home.

Outside, darkness is already blanketing the Brooklyn streets, and it only gets more menacing the longer I walk. Strange how I'm so close to where I live in Bushwick but I feel like I'm a world away. This area—what is this, East Williamsburg? Or am in Ridgewood, now?—is all warehouses, barbed wire, and parking lots. The closer I get to my destination, the fewer people I see, which is quite unusual in New York at any time, but even more so on a pleasant June evening like this one. It gets eerily quiet and the sound of my footsteps reverberates against the graffiti-adorned walls.

I feel a shred of fear. I'm about to meet up with a complete stranger. Anything is possible. But that only adds a kick of excitement. I've been doing this for four years. That's how long it's been since Cristian and I opened up our eleven-year-old relationship. The jitters, the thrill, it's all part of the game, isn't it?

Sometimes, I wonder what I would've done if Grindr was around when I was young and living in Chicago. Maybe I would've been too scared to use it, the way I was too scared to use pre-Grindr Internet chat rooms and forums. Never got into those. I was too afraid of the sexual deviants, the ones my uber-homophobic parents warned me about. Who knew that one day, from their point of view—and even from mine at the time—I'd become one of those myself.

For so many years, I'd been so afraid of my own desires. I'd jerk off—constantly—thinking about Jayden, the popular boy from gym class, or my buff American History teacher, and then cry from an explosion of guilt afterwards. I'd never look at the early, low-quality porn on the Internet for fear of leaving a trace. Eventually, yearning for what lay beyond the prison walls of my imagination, and no longer able to channel all my frustration into learning foreign languages, I found a dingy video store not far from Boystown. It took me three trips before I even mustered enough courage to walk inside. Then two more trips before I managed to actually buy anything.

The middle-aged video store clerk had many tattoos, including what I learned later was a Tom of Finland tattoo of an exaggeratedly masculine guy in a leather cap on his inner forearm. He intimidated the shit out of me. Handing him my choice of film, my entire body trembling, my breathing a shaky mess—*revealing* myself to someone like that for the first time—was one of the scariest things I've ever done in my life.

I was sixteen years old.

My internal struggle must've been evident to the clerk, who, technically, wasn't allowed to sell me any adult material. He studied me for a second, then rang me up like the military-themed gay orgy DVD was a pack of gum. I went back to that store dozens of times after that, buying discounted porn with my hard-earned cash from the Subway restaurant I worked at all throughout high school, and that man and I never exchanged more words than "thank you". A complete stranger saw me—the real me—and didn't judge. Saw my fear and my shame but didn't bring any attention to them, which was actually the best way for him to lessen both. How many other self-hating kids has he unknowingly helped the same way?

When I'm only a minute or so away from my destination, even the number of parked cars has dwindled. It's been a while since I passed a shop or restaurant, but the area doesn't look residential, either. There are zero signs of life, only empty factories and warehouses as far as the eye can see.

Before I reach the address the hot down-low guy sent me, I'm already full of dread, but it only multiplies when I actually do. The decrepit, low-rise building it corresponds to is as dark and deserted-looking as the ones that came before it.

Here, I tap into my phone. *Where are you?*

Nothing. Again, I check the guy's profile. It tells me that he's less than a hundred feet away and that he's currently online. I glance around but I don't see anyone. Unease flips my stomach. I follow up with a: ?.

Still nothing. But the guy is still online and nearby. Again, I look around. Again, not a soul in sight.

Just as I'm about to tell him I'm leaving, he sends me a message.

I see you, it says.

My eyes snap up. I scan my surroundings. No one. I look up, but the building's only window is dark, dirty and barred-up, and I don't see anyone watching me from the roof. I glance back at my screen to find another message.

You're handsome.

My skin prickles. In a flash, my heart is pounding with fear. *Dude*, I write, already turned around and walking back the way I came, *I'm out of here.*

Another message: *lol*

A surge of anger overtakes my fright. *Fuck you*, I reply.

Sometimes people on hookup apps are not who they say they are. But sometimes, you never even get to find out because they never intend to meet you in person at all. This type of shit has never happened to me personally, but I've heard stories. Men—or who knows who—leading you on, playing with you, getting a kick out of scaring you. Sometimes, it's a power game. And sometimes, it's pure cruelty.

The person doing this to me right now could be hiding somewhere, watching me at this very moment from some dark corner. But it's more likely that he's not even in the area. Or even in New York. He could be using some kind of software that allows him to torture me all the way from Florida or even South Africa.

At least, I hope the latter is the case, because the idea that someone is out there right now, watching me without my knowledge or consent makes my skin crawl.

I take one last look around. Nothing. But the piece of shit has sent me another message: *You'd do anything for some dick, wouldn't you?* it says. *Better be more careful, handsome. Dick's not worth losing everything over.*

I don't engage with the creep any further. Gritting my teeth, I hit the block button. The profile disappears. And, with it, so does the sadistic loser who wasted my time. Still, I pick up my pace. The entire way back to the station, I'm glancing over my shoulder.

Chapter 2

Not all potential hookups end in deception. Most are legit, and the best moment to let one know that you're happily married, in my opinion, is about fifteen minutes into meeting him in person for the very first time. By then, he'll have made the decision about whether he wants to fuck you or not, but won't be invested enough to get upset.

Tonight, however, is my second date with Russell Mailey and he still doesn't know about my husband. If Russell *asked* if I was single or if I was seeing anyone else then, of course, I'd tell him the truth. But he has yet to do that and, from what I know about him so far, I doubt he ever will. And if *he* doesn't care, I don't see why I should either. Four months from now, in September, Amelia is giving birth to our little girl and Cristian and I are officially closing up our marriage. So it's not like I can keep seeing Russell long-term anyway. And, honestly, I wouldn't want to, even if I could.

Physically, Russell's a stunner. I'm more impressed every time I see him. Only an inch shorter than my 6'2". Broad shoulders. Icy blue eyes. I'm a huge fan of the sexy strands of chest hair poking out of his always top-two-buttons-undone dress shirts.

"Hey," I say, sitting across from him at a fancy West Village restaurant. Surrounding us are dolled-up professionals on dates of their own, humongous trays piled with glistening oysters sitting between them. "Sorry I'm late," I add and lean over for an awkward kiss-hug combination. His beard tickles my cheek and I catch a whiff of his refreshing, citrusy deodorant.

"No worries," he replies, although his tone suggests otherwise. No surprises there. I bet not many people make the guy wait.

"How was filming?" I ask, because, as if his looks weren't enough, Russell Mailey is also apparently an in-demand television producer with his own production company and a show on Netflix. Even before he told me what he does, his name had sounded familiar. So he's not only hot and financially stable but also sort of famous.

"Ugh," he begins. "It was fine. Until Patricia showed up."

Unfortunately, Russell is much too aware of all the things he has going for himself and constantly makes a point to remind me and everyone else within hearing distance of how amazing he is. Which basically means he's a douche.

"That woman keeps forgetting," he goes on, "that if it weren't for me, there would *be* no filming in the first place."

Fortunately, the fact that he's a douche matters very little to me. What matters is that he's hot and famous and has lots of hot and famous friends. "You have no idea how many of the young hunks in Hollywood are secretly gay," he told me on our first date. "I'm buddies with most of them, just FYI."

I want to have sex with Russell and all of his famous friends.

Simple. Normally, I wouldn't be this shallow. But, I wouldn't be on a deadline either.

"Are you *sure* you can do it?" asked Cristian when we sat down to have the "return to monogamy" conversation, his bushy eyebrows—such a familiar, comforting landmark in my life—drawn together. "You can say no. I just think it might be best to give the baby one hundred percent of our attention. At least at first."

"And I *agree* with you one hundred percent," I answered with confidence. "I'll be fine. We've been closed before, you know."

"Yes," he said. "But that was before we were open. And you're not always the best at handling change, remember?"

"What?" I protested. "I totally am."

Cristian looked at me like: who do you think you're talking to? "So all those panic attacks you had when we were leaving Spain?" he asked. "I *imagined* those?"

Okay, fine. Maybe sometimes I overthink things and place a bit too much weight on the negative. I was happy in Spain. Or, at least, I was very content. I had a good job, spoke the language, I had Cristian. I was in control of my life. I was excited about New York and new prospects, and liked *the idea* of moving back to the States, but, even after we talked it through—and I mean *through*—I'd still get so lost in potential scenarios of doom— like, what if I never find a new job, or what if the move has a negative effect on our relationship?—I'd chew down my fingernails until I drew blood.

But we moved and I'm fine. More than fine, actually. It's been three years and I have a great position, Cristian and I have never been closer, and now, we're ready for a baby. Our life in

New York is everything we'd wanted and more. This time, it'll be okay too. The world's not going to end if, for a while, I cut out a few dicks from my life.

"Mi amor," I told him. "I promise you, it'll be fine. Besides, I'm Catholic for God's sake. I can do monogamy, trust me."

And so, at the end of the summer, when that monogamy comes, no more Russells, no more hookup apps, and no more random men and their cramped New York bedrooms. But, yeah. Until then, I intend to fuck as many guys as I can.

As annoying as it is, Russell's vanity kind of turns me on. I want to see that cocky smirk of his twisted into pure pleasure and, even better, maybe a little pain. I want to witness—and cause—that magical shift from arrogance to vulnerability that only happens during sex. I just really want to go there with him and I really hope tonight is the night. Because here's the real zinger about Russell Mailey: For all the markings of a fuckboy he may have, he has yet to do any actual fucking with me.

After our first date, after I listened to him brag about the huge Tribeca loft he has all to himself, I fully expected him to invite me over. But nope. Maybe his age has something to do with it? Unlike most of the some-form-of-younger guys that have been on my menu in the past—especially since Cristian and I agreed to close up—Russell is thirty-four, just like me. Maybe he's simply tired—or even bored—of the instant gratification on offer on the apps. Or maybe he just enjoys the build-up. Whatever it is, it's been fun, but I'm ready to close the deal.

"What are you doing Sunday?" he asks.

I clear my throat. "I'm, uh, seeing family in Westchester," I lie. Sundays are off limits. They're Cristian's and mine. Always have been and always will be. I change the subject. "When's your sister coming to town again?" I'm proud of myself for recalling the detail. I've been seeing so many guys in the last few months and at such a frequent pace their stories are starting to blend together. Sometimes, it's too difficult to keep track of who said what. Last week I said, "So is that why you went to Egypt?" to a guy who had specifically told me he didn't have a passport just a few minutes earlier.

As Russell launches into a soliloquy about his sister, because, with him, I've learned, everything leads to a soliloquy, I tune out his words and watch his lips move, imagining what they'd look like wrapped around the shaft of my cock.

"So you have or haven't?" he asks.

I blink. "Um, no, I haven't," I reply and his eyes instantly narrow with suspicion. This must be the wrong answer.

"Really? You're from Chicago and you've never had Italian Beef?"

Heat seeps into my face. Thank God for the dim light in this overpriced place. "No, of course I have. I was just kidding."

"What were you thinking about just now?" he asks, his tone interrogatory.

"Just, um, you know...*us*." It's not exactly a lie.

A small grin forms on his lips. Seemingly pleased with my answer, Russell looks into his wine glass and takes another sip.

As soon as both of our glasses are empty, ready to move on to the next stage of the evening, I call for the waitress. Having overheard the young, curly-haired girl speak the language to a customer earlier, I ask her for the bill in German.

After she makes some polite small talk with me and leaves, Russell says, "God, I still can't get over the fact that you're quadrilingual."

"I'm a translator," I reply with a shrug. "Languages are my job."

"But four?" he says, his head shaking. "English, Spanish, German, Chinese. *Chinese*! That's incredible. I'm super curious about your mind."

"Thanks," I say, surprised by the rare compliment on his part. I add a, "Likewise," even though the last thing that interests me about Russell is his mind.

The bill arrives. Internally, I cringe. Another drawback of going on so many dates per week is their regrettable effect on my bank account. At least with the younger guys, you can go to a dive bar, order a four-dollar beer and call it a day. With Russell's standard of living? Ouch—even when we split the amount down the middle. I need to be careful with my spending. Soon, I'll have to provide for a tiny, helpless human being.

On the way out, as we weave ourselves past candlelit tables, Russell graces me with a perfect view of his ass. It's firm, round halves push against the material of his dress pants in an almost obscene way. When we get outside and kiss, I can't resist giving it a good squeeze. He doesn't stop me so I push him up against a brick wall. My fingers pluck his shirt out of his belt, then sneak up his torso and wade through his chest hair to tickle his nipples. There's so much heat between us, I get bold and slip my hand behind his belt and inside the front waistband of his underwear where, for a brief moment, it grazes the base of his hard, restrained cock.

He pulls away, fixing his shirt. "Such a horndog," he says and fishes his phone out of his pocket. The light of its screen illuminates his bearded face.

Worry that this is as far as we'll get tonight speeds up my

heart. I move in and squeeze him again. "You bet your ass I am," I purr, pressing my crotch into his side.

He wriggles out of my grip. "My ass, eh?"

It dawns on me that I still don't know what Russell's preferred bunk is. "Yeah," I say. "Why? Not your thing?"

"No, I'm open," he answers, putting his phone away. A smirk forms on his lips. "I've just never bottomed before."

Blood rushes to my cheeks and makes my already hard cock even harder. "First time for everything," I say.

"Agreed," he replies. "With the right guy, of course."

"Of course." I point to my chest with both hands like "hello".

He snorts. "Stick around and who knows."

The way he says it, with hints of condition and finality, makes my heart sink. Still, I take my last shot: "Let's go to your place."

This time, he surprises me by pulling *me* into a kiss and grabbing *my* ass. My chest swells with hope. Again, my hands start to hungrily explore his body. But then he shoves us apart and looks toward the street where a black car has come to a halt. Turning, he starts in its direction. "Night, Greg," he says with a wink and slides inside.

CHAPTER 3

"Are we eating together today or do you have another lunch date?" Kate asks me at work the following day. I give her an apologetic wince and she crosses her smooth, deep-brown arms. "God, who is it today? The gorgeous Israeli boy again?"

"Nah, someone new."

"You're on fire lately!"

"That's the point," I say, swiveling my office chair to face her. "I only have the summer left to whore around, remember?"

Kate stretches out her hand. "Pics."

I pick up my phone from my desk and pull up a photo. I always make sure to save everything the guys I'm interested in send me, just in case. Other than a fleeting orgasm, photos are often the only souvenirs I get from our encounters and I like to remember the people I've swapped bodily fluids with. I'm a romantic like that.

Kate swipes the phone from my hands. "Jesus Christ," she says. "Look at those cheekbones." Her face tightens. She angles the phone my way. "His or yours?"

On screen, there's a close up of my erect penis. Heat rushes into my face as I yank the phone out of her hand and smack it face down on my desk. "Did I say you could go through the other photos?"

She shrugs. "It's nice either way."

"Thanks," I reply, blushing even harder. I'm comfortable enough with Kate to the point where no conversation topic is off limits, but I'm much less comfortable with her *seeing* exactly what my hard cock looks like.

"How did your date with the UPS delivery guy go last night?" she asks, my intimate photo a thing of the past.

"Last night was the TV producer."

"Okay, I can't keep track." She throws me a pointed look. "You know what you're doing, right? I know you like your boys but…too much of a good thing…"

I brush her off. "I'm just having fun."

"All right," she singsongs. "As long as it's not because you're freaking out about the baby and about becoming monogamous like you were last year about switching to the new translation management system."

I form my lips into a straight line. "I wasn't freaking out."

"Of course you weren't, hon."

Kate knows me too damn well. Sure, I'm a little worried. I'll admit it. Not about the baby—that part feels absolutely infallible. But I do wonder: Cristian and I may not be closing up forever but what if we actually are and we just don't know it yet? Or what if we're not but when we do open up again, I'll be in my forties or even fifties? Will guys still find me desirable? Will Cristian? What if, while we're closed, I lose my sex drive altogether? But these kinds of thoughts are perfectly normal. It's not freaking out and it has nothing to do with my—very occasional—anxiety. I know what I'm doing. More importantly, there's no harm in it whatsoever.

"*Anyway*," I say, ready to get back to the original subject, "the producer left me with blue balls again. That's why today's lunch date is extra important. I'm sure you understand." I show her my teeth.

Her eyes narrow. "Why are you trying so hard with this producer guy anyway?"

"I told you. He's hot. Plus, he's famous. Like, I think I've actually heard his name before I met him." I put on a grin. "He said that cute guy you like so much, the one who plays the detective on your little Hulu show, is gay. There's a party in a few weeks and he's supposed to be there. I'm hoping for an invite."

She scowls. "I fucking hate you."

"I hate you more."

After a quick scan of the office to make sure all our coworkers are still out of earshot, she asks, "How are things on the heteronormative family building front?"

"Fine," I say. "Cristian and I are having Amelia over tomorrow night. We'll cook for her—well, Cristian will cook—and then we'll watch a movie or something. It's supposed to help us bond with the baby. And give me an opportunity to spend more time with Amelia."

"You look extremely excited."

"You know how much Amelia and I love each other."

Kate laughs. "Well, you're stuck with her forever, so deal with it."

I can't pinpoint the exact moment Kate and I became this buddy-buddy. One day, she was the new Black girl with the dry sense of humor in the licensing department and the next, my

very own business-hours fag-hag. Soon after that, she was my best friend.

Sometimes, when I tell people I'm in an open marriage, they can't help cringing. They try to hide it but I can feel their biases shifting into gear. "Wow, this guy's selfish as fuck. He doesn't appreciate what he's got. He wants to have the cake and eat it, too." In the eyes of your average Jane or Joe, I instantly become the bad guy. That's why I don't tell a lot of people. But Kate's never judged me and I love her for that. She understands that relationships are complicated and take many forms because people are complicated. A part of me feels a tang of guilt for not eating with her today but it's not strong enough for me to cancel my lunch date.

Hooking up at lunchtime is the best. It's so efficient. If I can manage to cum at lunch, I can free up my evening and either spend the time I gain with Cristian or use it on a non-sexual date with someone new, which some guys—like Russell, I guess—require before putting out. On the rare occasion when I'm super horny, I can even cum again.

If I could, I'd have a lunch date every day until the baby but, alas, they're not as easy to come by as I'd like them to be. True, during the day the number of guys—especially younger guys— who can host at their apartments definitely goes up. If you work the evening shift bartending or waiting tables in the East Village and your roommate has a traditional nine-to-five finance gig on Wall Street, you have your place to yourself until he or she comes home. But finding attractive guys who can host *and* who are accessible during my flexible but still-officially-one-hour-long lunch breaks is not the easiest of feats. I'm willing to get on the train, but I usually don't risk going farther away than three or four stops.

Today's gentleman—Mathias is the name he gave me on Grindr—is blond, ripped, and based in Long Island City, which is only one stop away from Grand Central (where my office is) on the 7 train. I know the route is doable because I covered it at lunchtime last month to hook up with a young Korean father of three.

This is what I've learned about Mathias from all the texting I did with him this morning while my boss wasn't looking: He's a twenty-seven-year-old social media manager at some luxury goods company I've never heard of. He's off today because he had to work some luxury event over the weekend and he has his place to himself because his boyfriend (they're open, or so he claims) is at the office as usual. With his boyfriend, Mathias is exclusively a top but, as he said, he would be "down to bottom" for me. Considering that my sexless date with Russell last night left me obsessing about topping tops, I couldn't have asked for a more wish-fulfilling scenario.

Speaking of the devil, as I climb out of the subway at Vernon Boulevard in Long Island City, Russell sends me a text:

Out of town this weekend but want to come over to my place on Monday? I have an insanely expensive bottle of wine with our names on it.

Adrenaline explodes through my veins. Finally. He's finally ready to put out. Why else would he be inviting me over? I'm so excited I even let the douchey tidbit about the pricey wine slide without rolling my eyes.

Sounds great, I reply. *Looking forward!* I think about tagging on an eggplant emoji at the end but decide against it.

Above ground, midday pedestrians clog the sidewalks. It's

mostly young mothers pushing strollers and retired couples holding hands. I open Google Maps and focus on my destination. Once I'm heading in the right direction, I fire up Grindr, just to make my presence in the area known. I'm all set for today, and now for next Monday with Russell, but it's never a bad idea to plan ahead.

Five minutes later, after passing not one, not two, but *three* dog walkers—all towed by small armies of pooches of all shapes and sizes—I arrive at a red brick townhouse on one of the more picturesque blocks in the area.

Out in front, I text. *What apt?*

The three dots pulsate under my question.

Buzz 2.

As I climb the front steps, the nerves hit. In vivid detail, I recall the catfishing ordeal I went through just the other day on that dark, empty street surrounded by those menacing warehouses. The visceral fear I felt, the certainty that I pushed my luck too far. It all comes back to me. I'm about to be alone with a complete stranger in his completely strange apartment. Again, anything can happen.

On the second floor, the door swings open and the nerves quadruple. But not out of fear. Far from it. Out of surprise first and insecurity second. Because the shirtless man who greets me looks much better in person than he did in his photos.

This isn't exactly uncommon. It happens less often than the opposite, but it does happen. The problem is, it's never happened to me to this *degree* before. My husband is hot, and, like I said, Russell's a stunner, but this dude is on a whole other level.

The high cheekboned, Nordic-looking mountain of muscle standing before me smiles, but it's a reluctant smile so I give him a reluctant one in return, fully prepared for him to say "sorry" and send me back down the stairs where I came from.

"Come in," he says and steps aside.

I swallow and walk into his sun-drenched apartment, getting a good whiff of his body soap. He must've just stepped out of the shower.

Immediately, my gaze wanders over to the framed photos on his bookshelf. Three of them feature Mathias in various displays of intimacy with a gorgeous, dark-haired clone. This must be the boyfriend, I think, my stomach sinking, because if *that's* the person he's having sex with on the regular then he's definitely not having sex with me.

"Can I get you a water?" he asks. "A beer maybe?"

"A water," I choke up, stealing a glance at the silky treasure trail decorating his abs and the tantalizing gym-shorts bulge it leads to. Handsome, insanely fit, *and* considerate? "I do have to go back to work in a bit, unfortunately."

"You got it," he says, turning toward the fridge. My eyes latch on to the beautiful landscape of his back muscles, all the intricate ridges and valleys, which perfectly compliment the masterpiece in front. "So you're a translator?" he asks.

I clear my throat. "Yes. In-house. At this global IT startup."

He passes me a Poland Spring water bottle and says, "Very cool." I can't read his expression. I thank him for the water, twist off the cap, and down more than half its contents in one gulp. Come on, I think. Bring it on. I know you're out of my league.

"So where did you learn all those languages?" he asks.

"Mostly on my own," I answer. "I've always been a language nerd. While other kids played video games I was watching German TV and practicing writing Chinese characters in my notebook. My parents couldn't believe it."

Mathias smiles. "I wouldn't either."

"Then I studied them all in school at one point or another," I go on. "I also did a year abroad in Shanghai in high school and a year in Munich in college. After I graduated, I moved to Spain and spent most of my twenties living and working there."

"That's incredible," Mathias says.

"Thanks," I reply. His neutral, unreadable gaze is making me feel uncomfortable. I indicate the photos on the bookshelf. "Your guy's very handsome."

Redness seeps into Mathias's pale complexion. "Thanks."

"I'm in an open relationship, too," I add, immediately regretting getting on the topic of commitment in the first place. Nothing sexier than bringing up someone's partner when they're about to hook up with a stranger.

"Oh yeah?" he asks, his eyes growing bigger.

"Open *marriage*, actually. Been open for about four years now. Together for eleven though. We actually met when I lived in Spain."

"Oh, wow," he says. "You guys don't get jealous?"

And this is the moment I realize Mathias is probably *not* in an open relationship. The "you don't get jealous?" question is something you ask when you're curious about open relationships. Not when you're already in one. He probably just told me that because it was easier than having to hide all the photos in the house before I got here. "No," I reply, a lot less nervous now, "we don't." And I don't know why, but I feel the need to add: "We're having a baby in September."

He seems slightly flustered, but says, "Congratulations!"

"Thank you. I'm really excited." I pause. "But, yeah, we've

decided to close up again after our surrogate gives birth."

"Oh yeah?" He sounds disappointed. "Like, forever?"

"Probably not forever," I reply. "But definitely for a while. Without Grindr and all the random hookups we'll have more time to change diapers and stuff."

He doesn't laugh, just nods. "Makes sense. Are you staying in the city?"

"That's the plan."

A moment of silence follows, during which I'm not sure what to say and during which Mathias keeps staring at me.

"I think you're very handsome," he finally tells me. "You have this cool, masculine demeanor about you. The translator part already had me rock hard but now I find out you're going to be a father, too? So hot."

Holding my breath, I take a step toward him. Usually, I let the host make the first move; I'm a guest in someone's home, after all. But the clock is ticking and I don't want him to change his mind. I wrap my arms around his lower back—God, there's so much surface area to the guy—and pull him in. Our fronts connect. He feels solid everywhere, not just where his bulge is grinding against mine.

The bedroom door is open. I guide Mathias's giant mass toward it and push him onto his back. I yank off his gym shorts. His thick, circumcised cock slaps his perfectly flat stomach. Of course he has to have a beautiful penis, too.

All of a sudden, I remember I'm supposed to top. Now that the initial uncertainty over whether I'd even get to see this guy naked has been squashed, the pressure to perform squeezes me in its grip. I really wish that, before I left the office, I'd popped one of the Viagra pills I nabbed at a sex party three weeks ago.

To buy myself some time and to work my cock up to a more presentable size, I drop to the bedside and put my mouth to use. I suck him off for a bit before pushing his legs up in the air and sticking my tongue in his ass. His rhythmic moans and wrinkled forehead help me relax. My performance ends in success.

After the condom's disposed of and our bodies wiped clean, I begin to put on my clothes. "You don't want to shower?" he asks.

"No time, but thank you."

In the doorway, I turn to face him. We stare at each other and smile.

"I was really nervous when you got here," he reveals.

All I can do is scoff and shake my head in wonderment. Sometimes you get catfished and sometimes you hit the damn jackpot.

"See you again soon?" he offers. "Before you and your guy close back up?"

"Definitely."

We kiss goodbye.

On the way back to the office, I pick up a salad and replay the encounter in my head. I still can't believe a hottie of that caliber was into me. Next time, if there is a next time, I'll make sure to fully appreciate the artwork that is Mathias's body instead of wrestling with insecurities about my own. That kind of stress takes away from the fun and the point of these upcoming summer months is to have as much fun as possible.

Chapter 4

Cristian's phone pings. Over by the stove, he wipes his forehead with the back of his hand. "Mi amor, can you check that?" he says. "She's probably here."

I put the knife down next to the bell pepper I've been chopping and walk over to the coffee table. Sure enough, it's a message from Amelia announcing that she'll be arriving in front of our building in approximately four minutes.

"Can you go meet her outside?" Cristian asks once I relay this information.

"Of course," I reply, even though I'm sure Amelia would be just fine sashaying her almost six-month pregnant ass up to our first floor apartment without me watching her do it. In fact, I'm certain she'd prefer that.

Outside, I dash up to the car parked in front of our entrance and swing open the back door. Inside it, I find not the pregnant woman carrying my future daughter but two, already-born children with handheld gaming devices in front of their surprised faces.

"Can I help you?" the woman in the passenger seat protests.

24

"Sorry!" I say. "Wrong car!"

Embarrassed, I'm backing away when I spot Amelia clambering out of the mini-van standing a few feet ahead of the car I just assaulted.

"Greg," she says, approaching.

"Amelia," I respond.

"Is your buzzer broken?"

"No."

"Then why are you out here? Do you not trust me with the baby?"

I could tell her the truth and say: "Of course I don't trust you with the baby," but both she and I already know that. It doesn't need to be said out loud. I could also tell her that me coming outside was actually Cristian's idea—which might imply that *he's* the one who doesn't trust her with the baby—but I don't want to start the evening off on the wrong foot, either, so I just put on a tight smile and gesture for her to proceed.

Unlike Kate from work who, off the clock, often hangs out with both me *and* Cristian, Amelia has always been exclusively Cristian's friend. Technically speaking, I know Amelia for almost as long as I know him—that's to say, eleven years—and, technically speaking, there's been a coolness between us for just as long.

Originally from Wales, Amelia moved to Spain and married one of Cristian's good friends from art school. A couple of years later, she stopped being married to Cristian's friend and Cristian's friend stopped being Cristian's friend, but, somehow, Amelia remained in Cristian's life. And, as a result, in mine.

"Why does your stairwell always smell like rhinoceros regurgitate?" she asks.

"Don't know. Maybe one of your exes was in here."

"Hilarious."

The origin of our long-lasting tug-of-war has to do with Cristian. Because she's known him a couple of months longer, she thinks she's the ultimate authority on what's best for him, which, apparently, has never been me. At least that's my take on it.

"Ay, que preciosa!" Cristian says, giving Amelia a huge hug as soon as she steps through the door. Stirring spoon still in his hand, he falls to his knees and presses his face to her pronounced belly. She's wearing a white dress today, so the brown skin he inherited from his Dominican mother creates a striking contrast against it. Cristian does this every time, and every time, my heart still bursts with love. The sight is so sweet, even Amelia and I exchange a cordial smile.

As much as Amelia and I butt heads, I am grateful to the woman. I know for a fact that, for Cristian, she'd stand in front of a charging buffalo. And offering to carry our baby for free—well, Cristian's baby, biologically speaking, as we came to the decision to use *his* sperm for the artificial insemination—was a very generous thing of her to do. Of course, we're the ones covering all medical and legal expenses, and Cristian insisted on paying her a heftier-than-I-would've-liked stipend. She accepted the money, which is fine, but at the rate we've been making other, not-so-essential purchases on her behalf, I have a feeling we'll end up spending just as much—if not more—as what we would've spent had we gone the compensated way through an agency.

The thing is, Amelia never asks outright. That's why it bugs me. She'll be like, "Oh my back hurts, I think it's my sofa," and the next thing I know Cristian will be ordering her a new one from someplace like Design Within Reach. Most recently, it was a new, big screen television because the pregnancy was affecting her vision and she had trouble watching her favorite shows on the TV she had.

Cristian has always been generous, and I love that about him, but he's terrible at managing money. If it weren't for me, and my paychecks, we'd be drowning in debt and unpaid bills. And we certainly wouldn't be able to afford a two-bedroom in the heart of Bushwick. We're still on track, though, and I do want to keep everyone happy for as long as I can, so I've mostly been keeping my mouth shut.

"What else do you need me to help you with, mi amor?" I ask Cristian.

"Nada," he says, dashing back to the kitchen. I notice that the rest of the pepper I was working on is already in pieces. "Go sit with Amelia."

I shuffle over to the chair across from the sofa where Amelia is already lounging. Eyeing our living room with a disapproving grimace, she says, "You need to baby-proof this place." Her gaze lingers on Cristian's easel in the corner.

"I will," I say. "Don't worry."

She looks at me for a silent beat, blinks, and angles her face toward the kitchen. "Did you hear?" she says. "Vanessa scored a solo show in Chelsea in October."

"Really?" Cristian replies. "Where?"

Amelia continues carrying out a conversation with Cristian as if I'm not even there, but I actually don't mind. Cristian's an artist and Amelia's a graphic designer, so I'm used to being on the periphery of their art-related discussions.

Tonight, this also makes for the perfect opportunity to text back Russell, which I've been putting off for most of the day. Unfortunately, Russell's never-ending blah-blah extends to written communication as well. For every text from any other boy I've hooked up with lately, there are at least ten from Russell. If I want to fuck Russell and all of his famous friends, I have to reply to at least a portion of them.

From what I recall, he was last talking about his sister again, so that's where I expect to pick up, but now it looks like his one-sided conversation has shifted to his nephew, and, most recently, of all things, to children in general. Interesting timing with my surrogate sitting only a few feet away.

How do you feel about kids? his last text reads.

First, I apologize to him for not replying earlier and make up a lie about having a ton of translations to proofread for work. Then, with a smirk, I write: *I do like kids, yes. Wouldn't mind having some of my own one day.*

Russell replies almost instantly: *How many?*

Start with one and go from there.

That's the sexiest thing you've said since I met you.

I raise an eyebrow at the screen. Really? *This* is the sexiest thing I've said? Russell doesn't strike me as much of a father-type. Not in the way Cristian does. With Cristian, you see his gentle smile and the kind wrinkles around his eyes, and go, "this guy would make a wonderful father." You see Russell and think: "That guy would have no problem doing blow in front of my four-year-old."

Inspired, I ask, *What kind of drugs have you done?*

While the three dots pulsate, I glance up to make sure Amelia and Cristian are still engaged in a conversation that doesn't require my input. They are. My stomach grumbles. God, the ratatouille-like pisto Cristian's making smells delicious.

Marijuana, cocaine, mushrooms, and acid, I read on my screen. *But nothing in the past ten years. Been completely clean. As you know, I do like my whiskey, though.*

Again, I do a double take. There's no way Russell's this cookie-cutter. Why is he trying to make himself appear that way? Does he think that's what I want to hear? That it'll make him seem more appealing in some way?

And you? he asks.

All the ones you mentioned plus MDMA.

Any of them recently?

Yes. Two weeks ago, Kate's boyfriend, Hiro, brought some coke to our double date with Cristian, but Russell doesn't need to know that. *Nope,* I say.

Perfect.

Perfect for what, I think. *You have that Netflix party in two weeks, right?* I ask, changing the subject and hoping for an invite.

Yeah, he replies, but instead of inviting me, he transitions into an extended brag about his newest deal with Netflix. This is my cue to tune out.

"You know what I need right now?" Amelia is saying.

I tense.

"What?" Cristian asks, lifting our plates, which are topped with steaming chicken cutlets and vegetables. I shoot up to my feet and dash over to help him.

"Gracias," he says, passing them to me.

"I need a vacation, that's what," Amelia finishes. "Some sand and some saltwater. Ugh, that would do wonders for my anxiety."

Already, I know where this is going. "Pregnant women shouldn't really travel," I say, setting down one of the plates in front of her on the coffee table. "I don't think they'd even allow you on a plane."

"That's so not true," she says, dully, "and you know it."

"Are you sure?" I ask. "All that turbulence?"

Eyelids in half-mast, she gives me a look but, thankfully, moves on to another topic. Still, just as I expect, after we eat and Cristian and I finally see Amelia off to her Uber so she can get home, Cristian brings it up again.

"Maybe we should surprise her with a four or five-day getaway somewhere," he says while we clean up in the kitchen. "Turks and Caicos maybe? The less stress she goes through the better for our baby."

Sighing, I place a rinsed glass in the dishwasher. If I oppose the idea, I'll be opposing the health of our baby. "Why Turks and Caicos, though?" I grumble. "Mexico and Dominicana have sand and saltwater too. For much cheaper."

"That works," he says planting a kiss on my cheek. "Maybe you can take a few days off from work and go with her?"

The plate I'm holding under the faucet almost slips out of my hand. I stop what I'm doing and stare at him.

Cristian bursts out laughing. "I'm kidding, mi amor. But you really should make more of an effort to get to know her better. You're going to be the one picking up the breast milk after work, remember? Take her out to lunch or something this week."

"Without you?"

"Yes, without me."

I turn my attention back to the sink. With a small sigh, I say, "Fine."

Chapter 5

After work on Monday, on the train over to Russell's apartment in Tribeca, I make a lot of eye contact with an unusually tall, masculine-presenting Black guy wearing cute little glasses. I'm tempted to slide over and say hello.

The last man I talked to on the train ended up on his knees in a Barnes and Noble bathroom stall with me in it. I can easily envision Tall Dude partaking in a similar scenario, and based on the way he's looking at me, it doesn't seem that farfetched. Should I attempt a little detour before I get to Russell's?

I can only imagine what Cristian would say. *God, Greg. Do you ever not think about sex?* And, honestly, sometimes, I wonder that myself. You'd think the last detour I attempted, which ended in me getting catfished by some sadistic asshole on a dark empty street would deter me from making another one so soon, but you'd be wrong.

My libido has a life of its own. This is something I've known since puberty. And, since puberty, for a long time, I used to believe that what triggered it was the evilest of all evils. So what else could I do except suppress it with everything I had? But suppressing such a fundamental part of yourself takes its toll. Believe me.

When I finally came out at twenty-two—both officially to myself and the rest of the world—I made the decision that my sexual freedom would never be restrained again. That I'd have all the sex with all the men forever and ever until the day I died.

Then I met Cristian. At twenty-three. We became monogamous by default. My period of having sex with all the men forever and ever had only lasted about a year.

But that was okay because I loved Cristian and I was enchanted by him and monogamy was our entry point. But Cristian loved me, too. So much so, in fact, that he figured out, even before I did, that I was once again suppressing that big, uncharted part of myself. And he didn't want me to do that. So, he came up with a solution.

Most people assume that because I'm the one with the massive sex drive, and because I meet up with other dudes more often than Cristian does, that I must also have been the one to suggest Cristian and I open up. But that's not the case. True, Cristian probably did it more for my benefit than for his own, but he was the person who first brought the conversation to the table. On a few occasions before he did, I'd thought about it and maybe dropped a vague hint or two that it might be something I'd be interested in, but when push came to shove, I was too scared to actually come out and say it. I didn't want to risk disturbing what Cristian and I had. Cristian, however, it turned out, had as much faith in our relationship as I did. Maybe even more. And, being as generous as he is, wanted to make me even happier than I already was, if only by a little.

I got everything I'd ever wanted. An incredible partner

and a chance to make up for those dark stretches of my youth when I was so deep in the closet I thought sex—or at least the kind of sex I wanted to have, the kind that involves at least two penises—would remain unattainable to me forever. Now that I'm older and I've had my fill, there's another thing that I want even more: a child with my husband. A family. I'm more certain about this than I've ever been about anything else. I can feel it in my bones. And a period of monogamy, I believe, will help us, help *me*, make that a success.

So no, no detours for tall guys with cute glasses tonight. I really should start practicing some self-restraint. I'm going to be a father. And, anyway, I need to focus on getting only one guy on his knees tonight and that guy is Russell Mailey. Besides, I don't want to risk being late to our "insanely expensive" bottle of wine ceremony.

"You're late," Russell says when he opens the door to his enormous, high-ceilinged loft. I can't tell if he's joking or not so I just smile.

With Cristian, over the years, we've aligned to the point where one knows exactly what will make the other laugh and at what intensity. What will bring the other delight and what will make the other frown. The guys I hook up with, I can't read as easily. I don't want to risk saying anything that might piss Russell off, especially because this is the first time I'm seeing him in a T-shirt and gray sweatpants that leave very little to the imagination. I want to be taking steps *toward* getting inside those sweatpants, not away.

I step up to him and press our bodies together. While we kiss, I slide a hand over his ass. Past the soft fabric of his pants, it's firm to the touch. We make out like that for a minute before Russell disconnects himself and closes the door.

"Hi," I say.

"Hi," he answers.

I try to pull him back to me but he wriggles away and starts for the kitchen. I have no choice but to follow him and let the cold possibility that nothing sexual might happen between us sink in. Just because he invited me over tonight doesn't mean he's agreed to penetration. I can still hope but I have to play it cool.

Russell's gaze darts to my feet. "Shoes, please."

"Oh." I back up and kick them off. "Sorry."

"It's okay."

"Beautiful place," I say, taking in the industrial-style furniture, the giant windows and the illuminated cityscape beyond them. A lot of room for a child to play, I think to myself. The space is at least three times as big as Cristian's and mine.

"Thanks."

"So how many of those hot secretly gay actors have you had in here?"

From behind the kitchen island, where he's screwing a wine opener into the mouth of a slick, black bottle, Russell says, "Not many, unfortunately."

A handful of meticulously-framed movie posters—mostly highbrow indie staples—grace the tall, off-white walls. To my surprise, I spot a wooden cross hanging between the oversized windows. It momentarily reminds me of my childhood and my parents' home in Chicago, but also brings back those less pleasant memories of all the shame and sexual repression I experienced as a teenager. I shudder.

Another thing I notice is that, unlike my muscular, Nordic-looking hookup from lunch the other day, Russell has zero photos on display. An urge to ask him about his past relationships rises within me, but I squash it back down. That might lead to a turning of the tables and pressure me into telling him about Cristian, which I don't want to do.

"I know it might not seem that way," Russell goes on, "but I'm really not much of a hookup guy. I believe in love and romance and fate and all that other good old-fashioned stuff. I wasn't lying to you when I said that."

I don't recall him saying that but, to be fair, I do tune out a lot when he speaks. How can I not when he's so often just blowing his own horn? He doesn't limit his boasting to his accomplishments in the entertainment industry, either. He talks about how he knows doctors and lawyers and politicians and how they all owe him favors and whatnot. My instincts are telling me that this "I'm actually really wholesome" talk of his is all for show. But, then again, he hasn't slept with *me* yet, either, so maybe it's not all BS. "You are kind of an enigma," I reply, because, in certain ways, he really is.

"Believe it or not, back in the day, I was pretty shy."

"Really?"

"Really."

"Case of bullied gay boy blossoming into a powerful, suave man?"

Russell chuckles. "Something like that."

Running my fingers along the edge of the kitchen island, I maneuver around it. "Is that the expensive wine you were going on about?"

"Mmhm." He looks me in the eyes. "That's what we're here

for, isn't it?"

I deflate a little but try not to show it. "Sure is…"

He hands me a full glass. "My uncle's house on Nantucket is up for grabs next month," he says, his eyes locked with mine. "You in?"

Of course I'm not in. A romantic getaway to Nantucket with Russell? No thank you. But I raise my glass anyway. "I'm in."

He smirks. "How do you say 'great' in German?"

"You'd just say super…"

Less than a minute later, to my great relief, we can't get our hands off each other. My tongue is massaging the roof of his mouth. His hands are squeezing my pecs. I pull off his T-shirt—the citrusy scent of his deodorant sharpening—and then we're back at it again. I'm thinking: fuck yeah, but I'm also scared that, at any second, he'll pull away.

I slip my fingers inside the front of his sweatpants and wrap them around his warm cock. He doesn't recoil. Instead, he shoves his own hand in my jeans. Into his ear, I whisper, "Where's the bed?" still thinking this is as far as he'll let me go. But once again, I'm proven wrong. Russell starts leading the way.

We shuffle along, exchanging saliva, losing more clothes. When we pass thorough the doorway, Russell whips his head to the side. "Google!" he shouts. "Lights off!"

"No, no," I mutter. "Leave them on. I'm a very visual person."

He relents, orders Google to turn the lights back on. I try to kiss him again but his mouth jerks back. A burst of panic makes my already pounding heart beat even faster. We stand there, panting into each other's faces. "What?" I ask.

"I really like you," he says.

"I really like you too!" I lie.

Russell launches his lips forward and we're kissing again and, before I know it, he's shoving me onto the bed. We struggle like that, one trying to reaffirm his dominance over the other by getting on top. It's so primal, so red-blooded, so masculine. Like wrestling, or fencing, only instead of swords, we're using our cocks.

All of a sudden, while Russell has an advantage, he goes still. His hands have me pinned to the bed. He stares down at me with his icy blue eyes, his face hovering just and inch above mine. Jesus Fucking Christ, what now?

"I'm fucking you first," he says.

I snort with relief. "Fine. We can flip."

Looking deep into my eyes, he says, "Promise nothing's going to change?"

"I promise."

CHAPTER 6

Amelia's talk of sand and saltwater the other day only fueled Cristian's craving for the same things. Not that I'm surprised. Cristian grew up on the southern coast of Spain, not far from Málaga. Unlike me—Chicago's not exactly known for being a sunny beach destination—my husband has the sea in his blood.

New York might not have the turquoise waters of the Andalusian coast, but it does have serviceable beaches within easy reach. So, that Sunday, armed with tote bags full of snacks and towels, and branding a folded beach umbrella, Cristian and I take the train down to the Rockaways on the southern outskirts of Queens.

By day, Cristian manages an art production studio in Williamsburg for a fairly renowned Dutch artist. For some reason—possibly in accordance with the global tradition for cultural institutions—the studio is closed on Mondays. To make up for that, it's open on Saturdays instead. Since my job is a regular nine-to-five with the weekends off, Sundays are usually the only full days Cristian and I have to spend together.

"Did you talk to Amelia about hanging out?" he asks while

we wait to transfer to the A train on the platform at Broadway Junction. Below us, a pair of gargantuan rats skitter along the tracks and disappear into a dark crevice.

"Not yet," I answer. Between work and Grindr and seeing Russell again for an after-work quickie at his place on Thursday, I've had a busy week.

Sex with Mr. Producer is pretty hot, I have to say. Russell hadn't been lying when he told me he's never bottomed before. I loved the frightened expression on his flushed face when I pushed myself inside him. He's still super annoying when we're not fucking, but, Thursday, he did mention an upcoming private screening for some buzzy indie film and an even buzzier after party, so I'll hold out for a while longer.

"I'll invite her out to dinner this week," I say.

Cristian lowers his long eyelashes. "You better."

"Speaking of Amelia," I say, "I've been thinking…"

"Aha…"

"…and you know how we weren't sure what to get her after she gives birth?"

"Yeah…"

"Let's just get her that tropical getaway then. I'd really rather not have her flying and so far away from us." I stop short of saying: "And potentially being in a plane crash while carrying our unborn daughter."

Cristian thinks for a moment. Then says, "That works."

I smile. "Te quiero."

"Te quiero," he replies.

Once the baby comes, Cristian is set to take a pay cut and go to the studio he works at three days a week instead of five. For those three days, we'll hire a nanny to take care of our little girl.

I'd love to go part-time myself, but it wouldn't be the smartest idea from a financial perspective, as mine is the higher-paying job. And, more importantly, we'd risk losing our health insurance. Obviously, that's not an option.

Since it's June and summer in New York has only just begun, the beach is nowhere near as packed as it will be in the coming months. The sun is out and it's warm, but the air is still too brisk for my taste. But what do I know. Plenty of New Yorkers have already claimed their spots along the long, sandy coast of the urbanized peninsula. Rows of residential buildings at our backs, we get off the boardwalk and trudge toward the green-brown waves of the Atlantic.

"Let's go there," Cristian says, indicating an open stretch.

The second he puts down his bag, his shirt and the pants he was wearing over his swimming trunks are on the sand beside it. "I'll go check the water," he says with so much innocent enthusiasm, I wouldn't be able to protest and ask him to help me set up even if I wanted to. With a smile I nod and he runs off toward the waves.

Despite the European stereotype, Cristian does not wear speedos. If you ask me, it's kind of a disservice to everyone because he'd fill them out quite nicely, both in the front and the back. I watch him do a dive and wave to me when he resurfaces.

With those two extra days at home, Cristian will also have more time to work on his own art. It's something I'm really happy about. My husband has a master's degree in painting. He's made a few sales here and there, but he has yet to really take off, which, I have no doubt, will one day happen, even if he refuses to accept commissions and even if he only paints things he's passionate about. Our apartment's filled with his sweat and tears—paintings of people's faces, bodies, and, on occasion, their possessions. I love his style, especially his romanticized but still realistic interpretations of people in acrylic, and I'm not just saying that because I love him. The piece hanging on the wall in our bedroom—a self-portrait of Cristian sitting on the edge of the clawfoot bathtub we had in our old apartment in Madrid, his hairy thighs spread open, his hands unsuccessfully attempting to hide his privates—is my all-time favorite.

Cristian's skin may not be as taut and fresh as it is in that painting, and, these days, we may not have sex with each other for months at a time, but my husband still takes my breath away. The veins on his forearms, the large hands. The scattering of hair on his chest and belly. The overall, carefree masculinity he exudes even while standing still. Hands down, he's the hottest guy on this beach. I would know. I've already completed a thorough scan of all the other dudes in my peripheral field.

"Mierda," he says, strutting back to me, glistening beads of water sliding down his burly brown body. "I forgot to bring my goggles."

Reaching into one of the tote bags, I dig around until my fingers find the things. I take them out and dangle them in the air. A huge smile erupts on Cristian's face. He leans down to give me a kiss but I have to cut it short as he's completely wet.

While Cristian once again turns into a sexy, Spanish merman, I pull out my new celebrity memoir about fatherhood. But before I start reading it, I check my phone.

Unsurprisingly, there's a new message from Russell. This time, he's sent me...his favorite quote? And it appears to be something about destiny from the bible. Wow. At least he managed to surprise me? I disregard the text and move on to Grindr.

The sun makes it difficult to see what's on screen, but I do succeed at sending some "hey" conversation starters—which I intend to pick up when I'm alone and have better reception—to a couple of nicely sculpted Rockaway area torsos.

Putting the phone away, though, I feel a sting of guilt. Today should be about me spending time with my husband. I can't even go a few damn hours without looking at Grindr? My period of non-monogamy is not the only thing with a deadline on it. So is my one-on-one time with Cristian. Once the baby comes, it'll never again be just the two of us, not really, for a long time. Not until our daughter is an adult. And also, how would I feel right now if Cristian was over there on his phone doing the same thing?

I squint against the sun and look for him. But I don't spot him mid-breaststroke in the water where I expect him to be. Instead, he's sitting just down the beach, surrounded by three small kids and two adult women. It looks like he's in the process of leading the construction of something in the sand. His rich voice, mixed in with the children's squealing, drifts over on the salty-smelling breeze.

Cristian's magnetism is legendary. Unlike me, he's extremely approachable. All he has to do is smile and everyone within a fifty-foot radius wants to be his friend. I don't talk to random people unless I want to sleep with them. Cristian talks to everybody. Constantly. Thankfully, I've had plenty of time to get used to that.

In many ways, Cristian and I are opposites: I tend to think with my head, he with his heart. I grew up in a cold place, he did not. Even physically, I'm on the pale side and he's full of melanin. But maybe this is why we've managed to stay together as long as we have. We've been complementing one another for eleven years and through different stages of our lives. Our relationship is a quilt of common firsts. Together, we got to marvel at the massive medieval town square in Krakow for the first time. Together, we got our very first tastes of poke and escargot. Together, we cried when cancer took his dad and celebrated when I got my big bonus at work.

And now, together, we're about to enter the world of parenthood.

I weigh down our blanket with our bags so the wind doesn't send it flying, give the shady-looking seagull lurking nearby the eye, and head over. Normally, I'd let Cristian be Cristian and go back to my book, but the children—especially the moon-faced little girl, no older than a year and a half—are too adorable to ignore.

When I say hello, she dismisses me with an uninterested glance and returns to piling more grains of sand onto Cristian's deformed castle thing with her tiny, chubby hands. I crouch down to pretend to help, but the girl's indifference shifts to annoyance so I immediately retreat. She's unbearably cute even when she's mad. I exchange a knowing smile with Cristian and stand back up.

I say hi to the women as Cristian proceeds to explain, in Spanish, who I am and who Amelia is and when we're expecting our daughter because, as usual, he has zero qualms about telling randos all of our business. The women—particularly the shorter lady wearing an oversized Tweety Bird T-shirt and sporting an unmistakable resemblance to the adorable little girl—demonstrate flashes of confusion before they fully comprehend what he's saying and begin to lavish us with congratulations. Unfortunately, as they do, they're not very successful at hiding their disappointment.

Sorry, ladies, I think to myself. I know he's hot, kind, and great with kids.

But he's mine.

CHAPTER 7

Wednesday, I'm convinced I'm spending the evening with Cristian when, at 5 p.m., just as I'm about to leave work, he surprises me with a text in which he announces that, tonight, he's going out on a date of his own.

Usually, when he has plans with someone, he gives me a bigger heads up, so, at first, I'm a little disappointed. I was looking forward to maybe meeting up with him in the West Village and walking our usual route down to Essex-Delancey before getting on the train back to Bushwick, where we'd top the night off with some take-out and TV. I thought we might even watch that new documentary about babies and communication. But it's all good. All of that can wait. Cristian's entitled to some fun, too.

I text him back: *Okay, what time do you think you'll be home?*

He replies with, *I don't know...Ten-ish?*

My heart speeds up. When Cristian says ten-ish, he means eleven-ish. Maybe even twelve-ish. For the next few hours, I can have our apartment to myself. A weeknight opportunity like this one rarely presents itself.

Officially, we're not supposed to bring any men back to our apartment. A year prior to leaving Madrid, when we first opened up the relationship, Cristian and I created a "no randos in our bed" rule that didn't allow it. But for a while now, especially in the time since we put a deadline on our non-monogamy, I've broken this rule quite a few times. What? Sometimes, rules need to be amended. Hosting in New York, where everyone has a gazillion roommates, can be a logistical nightmare.

Obviously, because he's not an idiot, Cristian's well aware of what I've been up to. The first weekend after we put a stamp on our decision to close up, he found a wristwatch on our windowsill. Neither of us owns a wristwatch. He didn't get mad though. He didn't even speak. He just sighed and put it back.

Still, I felt guilty. That's why, these days, I like to at least give homage to our little rule by being as discreet about my at-home hookups as possible. I do my best to dispose of all evidence—guest towels drying in plain sight, condom wrappers sitting in the trash bin—before Cristian gets home.

Because the last guy I slept with was Russell, the first person my mind conjures up for tonight is him. He'd be over in a blink, too. Today alone he's already sent me four texts, three of which I have yet to reply to. But nah, no Russell tonight. I don't really want him in my home. And, unless I'm willing to finally let him know about Cristian, I'd need to make the apartment look like it doesn't belong to a gay couple expecting a baby. Most importantly, though, tonight, I'd rather have something less complicated.

On the train home, I text one of my old regulars, Ian, a *What's up*, expecting him to reply with a *Chillin'*, because that's what he does every time I reach out.

A minute later, *Chillin'*, is exactly what I get.

Have the house to myself tonight, I write and tack on a grinning purple devil emoji, just in case my intentions aren't clear enough.

Come to mine, he replies.

My shoulders slump. Going to Ian's place would mean fucking in his dark, cramped bedroom with his unwashed German Shepherd sticking his wet snot everywhere and humping everything in sight.

I'll call you an Uber, I say and hit send. *Both ways*, I add.

He responds with: *K*.

It doesn't get any less complicated than Ian. He comes over. He fucks me. He leaves. The most complicated part is the enema I have to give myself beforehand.

Ian is a total top. The dude has a panic attack if you as much as brush a fingertip anywhere near his asshole. Not that I'm complaining. It's actually thanks to Ian that I know what being on the receiving end of a good dicking-down is actually like.

Before him, I used to think of bottoming as a chore. I didn't hate it but I didn't like it, either. It was just something that needed to be done. On top of that, Cristian had always preferred to bottom, so I went on with life thinking I was meant to be a top. Then Cristian and I opened up the relationship, Ian came along, and it turned out I was always meant to be a bottom, too, I just didn't know it yet.

I take one last peek in the bathroom mirror and move over to the couch. Uber tells me Ian will arrive in six minutes.

While I wait, I fire up Grindr to make sure I'm not missing out on anything else because, these days, I get dick FOMO even when I'm about to have some. To my relief, none of the guys who've hit me up since I was last on are my type.

As I scroll around, Grindr informs me that I have a new message.

Hi, the new message says. I check who it's from only to be greeted by a familiar-looking torso. For a couple of seconds, I stare at it. I'm sure I've dealt with its furry abs before. I'm trying to figure out when and where exactly when I receive a follow-up message from the same person: *No wonder you're not replying to my texts*, the follow-up says. *You're obviously very busy.*

This is when it hits me. The torso. It's Russell's.

A chill creeps up my spine. Russell and I met on Tinder. I've never seen him on Grindr before. Creepier still, Grindr is a location-based app. Most people use it to find guys who happen to be nearby. Russell lives all the way in Tribeca, which means he specifically sought me out, targeting my area.

A text from Ian lights up my screen: *Here*, it says. I toss my phone onto the coffee table and dash over to the intercom to buzz him in.

The first thing Ian does when I open the door is pop his chin up in greeting. My lips set into a smile as I do the same in return. It's been over a month since I last saw the guy. I realize how much I've missed him.

"'Sup," he says.

"'Sup," I reply.

Ian's not particularly handsome, nor is he particularly fit. He's twenty-five but he's already losing hair at the top of his head. To see the thinning area, you have to look down at his head directly from above, which maybe not many people get a chance to do, but I get a perfect view every time he's sucking my cock. The bald spot doesn't bother me. In fact, I kind of like it. Ian might just be average in appearance—and that's if you're generous—but his confidence makes me harder than any old six-pack.

Off the bat, he kicks off his sneakers and struts over to my coffee table to empty out his pockets—phone, earphones, keys—like he owns the place. In the middle of my living room, he proceeds to strip off his pants.

"That's a new one, isn't it?" He points to one of Cristian's paintings. It's a new acrylic piece Cristian had just finished, from memory, of his late grandmother.

"It is indeed," I reply, unable to take my eyes off the slit in Ian's boxers.

"I like it," he says through the material of his T-shirt because that's coming off too. "The old lady looks badass. I think I prefer it to the bathtub one."

"Nah," I say, visualizing Cristian's naked form hanging in our bedroom. "The bathtub one's the best."

"What would I have to do to get your man to paint a portrait of me?" Ian asks.

I snort. "A lot. I've known him for eleven years and he has yet to do mine."

"Really?" Completely naked now, Ian stands before me. His already hard—decently-sized and perfectly straight—cock is pointing right at the tent in my own shorts.

"He's taking his time," I say, playfully. "He loves me too much."

"Yeah," Ian teases, "or not enough."

I laugh. "Shut up and get over here."

Knowing I won't have many opportunities to kiss him, I move fast to connect our mouths. With Ian, barely any kissing happens when we fuck, and he absolutely refuses to kiss me after he cums. "To be honest," he explained to me one time, "once my hormones stop flowing, kissing dudes kind of disgusts me."

When it comes to longevity amongst my fuck-buddy regulars, Ian is the reigning champion. About a week after Cristian and I moved to New York, Cristian was in Chelsea having dinner with a friend from art school and I was on Grindr. It was an exciting time. Cristian and I had only been open for a year, we'd just gotten married after moving to the States, and we'd just made a new home in the greatest city on earth.

Ian sent me a "'sup" and an hour later I was saying hi to his roommates and playing tug of war with his dog, Wilbert. In his messy bedroom, we split a joint and, after a few failed attempts on my part to get to his ass, he fucked me like no one had ever fucked me before.

Today, he fucks me for just under an hour. I know exactly how long it takes because while he's showering, I check my phone to see if I have any updates from Cristian. Ian probably could've kept railing me for an hour more, but it's a weeknight and, just as I suspected, Cristian will soon start making his way home.

After his shower, still half-wet, Ian struts over to the refrigerator, dick swinging. He plucks out a bottle of orange juice and makes his way over to the couch. "So what's up?" he asks, falling onto it and draping an arm over the backrest.

"Same old," I say, lifting a freshly opened beer to my lips. "Oh, Cristian and I have a little baby girl on the way. Not sure if I told you."

"Well, shit!" he says. "Congrats, buddy."

"Thanks."

"That explains the ultrasound photo on your fridge."

"Yeah," I say with a laugh.

"And the books." He glances at the open one perched face-down at the end of the couch, the one I was reading last night about nurturing your child's developing brain.

I nod. I think about telling him that I'll have to stop seeing him when the baby arrives, but this doesn't quite feel like the right moment.

"That's a big step," he says. "You scared?"

"A little," I answer. "But I think it's time."

The bottle of juice he's drinking lifts into the air. "Right on."

"What about you?" I ask. "What's new with you?"

"I'm moving to LA in a week."

I blink, surprised. I fully expected him to say "same old," like he usually does. Not to reply with a life-changing decision. "Oh," I say. "That's...soon."

"Yeah. Good thing you hit me up."

"Are you going there for work?"

"My fiancé's work."

"You have a *fiancé*?" I do recall Ian mentioning a girlfriend once or twice. But when did she turn into a fiancé?

"Yeah," he replies.

"Same girl?"

"Yeah."

For a moment, we just stare at each other. And while we do, a strange, bittersweet feeling settles over me. Here's a guy with whom I've had countless intimate encounters. A guy who opened me up to new carnal pleasures. Someone who knows things about me no one else knows, done things to me no one else has, not even Cristian. Yet we have only ever really existed to one another when we were in each other's presence. I realize I don't even know his last name.

CHAPTER 8

The West Village bar Russell tells me to meet him at this time is filled to the brim with Russell clones—attractive, clean-cut men in their thirties, shirt sleeves rolled up, manly "on the rocks" types of drinks on the tables in front of them. Many sit across effortlessly attractive, long-necked women in their twenties.

I'm not thrilled about the fact that I'm in a bar at all. For obvious reasons, I'd much rather be meeting Russell at his apartment again. I suggested as much but, alas, he wouldn't have it. It's fine, though. As long as we end up at his place at some point tonight, I'm willing to endure another date with his ego. But if this one doesn't get me any closer to an official invite to that upcoming buzzy film screening and after party he told me about before, it might have to be our last. My patience for Russell and my time of non-monogamy are both running out.

Plastering on a smile I make my way over to the far end of the bar counter where he's saving me a seat. "Hey, stud," I say and settle in beside him.

"You're actually on time today."

Something in me flares. "Am I? You're kind of anal about

that shit, aren't you?"

He shrugs. "When you agree to be somewhere at a certain time, I expect you to be there at a certain time. Am I wrong? Don't say it if you don't mean it." His blue eyes pierce mine. "I'd say that applies to pretty much everything."

I feel a pinch of guilt. *I really like you, too.* I drop my gaze to the counter. "So," I say, scanning the drink menu. "How was work?"

Russell starts complaining about an actress who couldn't remember his name at a meeting. I manage to listen for five whole minutes before reaching my limit and sliding my hand up his thigh. Bringing my cheek up to his, I say, "I want to fuck you so bad."

Under my hand, I feel his muscles stiffen but he doesn't stop talking. He just removes my hand from his thigh and entwines it in his own.

"Let's get out of here," I try again.

"I think I'm going to order some food."

"Let's order in."

He lifts his gaze from the food menu and looks me dead in the eyes. "I don't want to have sex tonight, Greg."

I sit up straighter, withdrawing my hand from his. "Oh…."

"We don't have to have sex every time we see each other," he continues.

"Every time?" I force a chuckle. "We've had sex twice."

He shrugs and returns his attention to the laminated menu.

"Well," I say with a sigh, "I *do* want to have sex tonight so…."

His face snaps up. "So what?"

"So maybe we should call it a night."

His jaw clenches. "Are you serious?"

It's my turn to shrug.

"Really? So you're just going to leave? And what? Fuck someone else?"

"I didn't say *that…*" Although, yes, of course that's the plan. I'm already thinking about making a pit stop at one of my regular's apartments on the way home.

"No," he says, "what you said was that nothing would change. You *promised.*"

"What?" I start, feeling my blood pressure rising. "Look, sex is pretty important to me. Why are you so against it anyway?"

"I'm not against anything. I just don't want to make it the focus of our relationship."

A snort flies out of my nose. "Why not?"

"Because I want to get to know you better? Because I want this to *work*?"

"Get to know me better?" I ask. "And how are you planning to do that? You talk about yourself for ninety percent of our conversations."

He glares at me. "Is that so?"

I glare back. "Yes, that is so."

He angles his body towards mine and crosses his arms. "Well, then, talk to me," he says with a shrug. "Tell me something I don't know about you."

"Okay," I say. "How about this: I'm *married.*"

My heart is hammering but Russell just keeps staring at me, as if he didn't even hear me. I wait for his eyebrows to knit together, for him to demand an explanation. But he doesn't. None of that happens. Instead, in the most matter-of-fact manner possible, he shrugs and says, "Yeah. Cristian Torrero. I know."

A shiver runs over my skin. "What?"

"You're married to Cristian Torrero."

"How do you know that?"

"Marriage info isn't exactly secret information."

Disoriented, I shake my head. "And so what? You're okay with that?"

"Yeah," he says. "Because you're not actually together, are you?"

I scrunch up my face. "Huh?"

"You're married but you're not together. Either that or you don't love him anymore and want to leave him." He pauses. "Otherwise, you wouldn't be doing this," his hand glides back and forth between us, "with me, right?"

"We're in an open relationship."

Russell flinches. "So… you're happy? And you *want* to stay with him?"

"Of course! We're having a baby in, like, three months!"

His gaze slides down to his beer. His hand grips the base of the glass. "I assumed it was over. Or that it was just a green card marriage or something."

I snort. "Why would you assume that?"

His breathing intensifies. "Because people who are in successful open relationships are usually *open* and *honest* about being in open relationships," he says. "They don't *deceive* other people."

"I didn't deceive you. You never asked and it just never came up."

"What a coincidence!" he says. His volume has considerably increased. "We have sex—where I let you *fuck* me, by the way, something I've never let *anyone* do before—and now it magically does. Now it does come up." A nearby straight couple has stopped talking and is now sneaking glances our way.

"What do you want me to say?"

He scoffs. "You're not even going to try to deny it?"

"Deny what?"

"So you agree that you made me believe that a future with you was possible just because you wanted to fuck me?"

A tsk slides off my tongue. "Oh *come on*, Russell," I say, my volume rising too. "This wasn't even close to serious and you know it."

Spit flies out of his mouth. "You're a fucking prick."

A tired sigh leaves my lips. "Okay, dude, we're obviously not a match. We're looking for different things."

Russell goes quiet, his lips pinched, his nostrils flaring. When he opens his mouth again, he's oddly calm. "You think you know me? Know what I want?"

I hold his gaze. "I know enough."

He nods and turns away.

"I'm sorry, Russell," I say, sliding off my stool. "Take care."

He doesn't move.

At the exit, I take one last glance in Russell's direction. His expression is contorted into a mix of disgust and anger. But there's something else in it, too.

Is he...? Oh my god, is he *crying*?

Confusion unfurls in my chest. Russell's all arrogance, strength. He's not a crier. I consider walking back over there to ask him if he's all right, but I have a feeling that would only make things worse.

I don't realize how emotionally drained—and un-horny—I am from the experience until I sit down on the train. I guess I'll make a pit stop at a fuckbuddy's place another time. Tonight, I just want to go home.

But why the hell do I feel so *guilty* all of a sudden? Russell is an entitled douche. So what if he cried a little? He can't handle getting dumped by a guy he only hung out with a handful of times? What is he, fourteen? I'm not going to overthink this and let my anxiety get the best of me. I handled that situation just fine. God, I'm so glad to be closing up my marriage. I'm getting too old for this shit.

In Bushwick, when I get out of the station, huge pellets of rain start pouring down from the night sky, pummeling my clothes and skin. By the time I'm at my door, stabbing my key in my lock, I'm soaking wet.

Cristian—in his trademark pre-bedtime attire of thick glasses, a plain white T-shirt and striped pajama bottoms—glances up at me and smiles from where he's mixing paint on the couch. The news, in Spanish, is blaring from the TV. "You're drenched," he says. When he sees my long face, a wrinkle forms on his forehead. "What's wrong?"

Shaking my head, I start to carefully peel off everything the rain touched. "Just…a long day," I reply. With a towel, I get myself relatively dry and fall to the couch beside him. I give him a kiss and rest my head on his shoulder.

"Date didn't go so well?" he asks.

"You could say that," I mumble.

Cristian plants a peck on the top of my forehead. He doesn't ask where I've been or who the date was with. He never does. Not even these past few weeks when I've been spending so many evenings outside our home. As long as I inform him ahead of time when I'll be out and when I'll be home, he's happy.

I can't say that's the case for me. I've stopped interrogating

Cristian with as many questions as I used to, but I still like to at least *inquire* about who he's hanging out with. Sometimes, I stalk his guys on Instagram, just to see what they're like.

One of his long-time regulars, Danny, is some sort of photographer. On his Instagram, among the dozens of snapshots of New York City, he only has four photos that feature his face. Of those four, only two are non-artistic enough to tell me what he actually looks like. I guess he's cute, but Cristian could do better.

"I've got a date tomorrow too, don't forget," he tells me.

I nod. "Danny?"

"Joseph," he replies.

That's another guy Cristian's fond of. Only Joseph doesn't have a social media presence at all so he's even more of a puzzle. All I know about Joseph is that he owns a quaint Italian restaurant in Ridgewood. Once, I asked Cristian why he wouldn't indulge my curiosity and tell me more about him, maybe even introduce us.

"What's the point?" Cristian answered.

"I ask you about your painting, don't I? It's the same thing. I'd gain more knowledge about you. About who you are and what you like."

"It's not the same thing," he replied. "Not everything in life has to intersect. Besides, I know you. You'd only get jealous."

"I would *not*," I said, but my voice didn't carry much conviction because, okay, there was a time when I kind of did get jealous.

When we first moved to New York, it bothered me that Cristian would spend so much time with Danny and Danny alone. I couldn't comprehend why. He could've been meeting up with all these new people, but no, he just kept hanging out with the first New Yorker he went on a date with. It didn't make sense to me and my anxiety was spiking.

"We only hooked up a few times," Cristian told me when I accused him of having feelings for the guy. "We're friends, first and foremost. Sex is secondary."

"Then what the hell do guys *do* together?"

"We *talk*. Jesus Christ, Greg, not everything's about sex!"

Now I know that being in an open marriage can mean different things to different people. Sometimes, even to the two people within one.

Anyway, Cristian may not like to talk about his dudes, but I like to talk about mine. I want him to know how hot or how dumb a guy I hooked up with was in the same way I want him to know how funny that thing Kate said at work was. I want to share my experiences with my husband, whatever they may be.

But not tonight. Tonight, I don't tell him about my evening with Russell. Maybe another time I will, but, now, I just want to forget all about it.

CHAPTER 9

Usually, since, on Saturdays, Cristian's at work until 6 p.m. and I have the day to myself, I might use it to go to the park if it's nice out, or lounge around on the couch and put on a Spanish-language film or two if it's not.

These past few weeks, however, I've mostly been using the time to host.

That's the plan for today as well. But, today, before I bring a boy back to our place, I'm taking said boy to brunch.

I say "boy" because today's candidate, Elijah, is twenty-two. When he first hit me up last night with his *very* tempting photos, I immediately sent him my location and suggested he come over directly. Alas, he told me he prefers to meet out in public first. But I respect that. Besides, it *is* a great day for brunch.

I arrive just in time to see Elijah climb out of the subway. His plain gray pocket T-shirt is neatly tucked into his elegant, white trousers. You'd think that his muscular, wrestler-like frame would be better suited to a football uniform, or at least athletic wear, but it looks like the boy knows how to complement it with classy clothes.

He sees me past his lightly-tinted sunglasses and beams out a radiant smile. I extend a hand. "Pleasure to meet you, Elijah."

"Likewise, Mister Greg."

While I lead him to a favorite Asian fusion restaurant on Wilson Ave, I discover how polite and quick-on-his-feet he is. Chic fashion sense aside, his features, by themselves, give off a thickheaded bro type of vibe. But once he smiles or opens his mouth, he turns into a sweet, inquisitive all-American boy.

All over Bushwick, people sit on their stoops. Some with hipster brands of bottled beer in their fists, some blasting mariachi music from the speakers of their wide-open cars, but of all of them basking in the warmth of the sun.

"I love this neighborhood," Elijah says.

"Me too," I reply.

"Do you live by yourself?"

My ears get hot. "No, I do not."

"You're married, Mister Greg, aren't you?"

I do not expect this. I thought *I'd* be the one pointing out my marital status to him. And after what I've been through with Russell, I've *definitely* been planning to point out my marital status to him as soon as possible. "I am, yes," I reply with a nervous chuckle and glance at him to gauge his reaction.

There's a weak smile on his lips. "I figured you might be."

"Oh yeah?" I ask, aware that this date might now be in free fall. Dealing with men in open relationships is not everyone's cup of tea but I really hope it is Elijah's. I know the kid for less than twenty-four hours, but from what I've gathered about him from our texts and the brief time since we met up, I like him and I want him to like me.

"Yeah," he says. "You're in your mid-thirties, you're handsome, in shape, you're funny, you have a cool, stable job. There's no reason you'd be single."

"Oh, wow," I say, feeling myself blush a little. "Thank you for that. But I do understand if, um, me being married is…" My chest tightens. "…a deal breaker." As much as I want to hook up with him, the kid deserves respect.

When Elijah's eyes meet mine again, there's a determination in them that convinces me he's about to turn around and head back to the subway. But his smile only brightens. "It's not," he tells me and I breathe with relief.

After brunch, we get iced lattes and claim one of the last empty benches at Bushwick's premier green destination, Maria Hernandez Park. The giggles of children waft into our ears from behind. Every minute or so, a jogger drifts past us in front. Elijah starts talking about a movie which I haven't seen, but which, coincidentally, stars an actress I recall Russell mentioning in one of his never-ending diatribes. I shudder at the memory of Russell and re-focus my attention on Elijah. God, the kid's skin is so vibrant.

"Do you have a thing for older guys?" I blurt, apropos of absolutely nothing he's currently talking about. I only feel stupid for a second though, because this is something I've been genuinely wondering about since he reached out to me on Grindr. I do believe that, to an extent, age doesn't matter. But in this case, there's twelve years between us. That's practically the entire length of my relationship with Cristian.

When I think back to when I was twenty-two, having Saturday brunches and dick appointments with thirty-four-year-old men was definitely *not* on the itinerary. That was the year I came out after a long and deep time in the closet. Still, even after I loosened up and started fucking around—at first in the States for a while, then briefly again in Spain before I met Cristian—guys over thirty were either family or strangers to me. Never anything in between. I know it's a different world now, with dating apps and social media. People, from different ages and backgrounds are much more connected now, much more exposed to one another. But, to this day, it's still hard for me to shake the suspicion that there's something else behind this type of attraction.

Elijah laughs. "Hmm," he says. "I do *like* older guys, for sure. But my first boyfriend was my age, so I think it just depends on the person."

"What is it that you like about older guys?" I ask.

He thinks for a second. "Confidence. Stability. Older guys know what they want. Oftentimes, they already have it. I find that attractive. Most guys my age have no idea what they want." He puts on a grin. "Also, they're bad at sex."

Personally, I'm not sure I agree with that last one—I think sex is a lot like dancing: you either have a knack for it or you don't—but I nod like I agree anyway.

Elijah's hand travels up to the side of my head. It's the first time he touches me since our handshake and I'm zapped with a delightful tickle of electricity. "And I like *this*," he says, fondling the gray hair at my temples. "This is extremely hot."

"It's barely visible," I mumble.

"It's *pretty* visible," he says.

"Shut up."

After a chuckle, he asks, "Do you have a thing for younger guys?"

"Not exclusively," I reply.

"How old is your husband?"

"He's a year older. Thirty-five."

"And what about your boyfriends before him?"

"I didn't really have any boyfriends before him. Not long-term ones, at least. I've been with Cristian for eleven years."

Elijah's face softens. "Aw. That's kind of romantic."

"I guess."

"Is that why you wanted to open up the relationship?" he asks. "Because you didn't have much single time in your life?"

I feel myself blush. This kid's perceptive. "Well, *he's* the one who suggested we open up," I say. "But, yes, mostly because he could tell that I wanted to."

"He didn't?"

"Hmm," I say. "He claimed he did. But probably not as much as me. If my libido is at one hundred, his is at less than a quarter of that. But I was too scared to mess with what we had. So I mostly stayed quiet until he brought it up."

"But it turned out fine in the end, right?"

"Absolutely." I smile. "I'd say it turned our relationship into an even better, deeper bond than it originally was."

"Yeah," he says, nodding to himself. "Romantic for sure."

Our conversation drifts from topic to topic. He tells me about his upcoming trip to Brazil, which leads to a dialogue on travel. We discuss how we feel about our president. I tell him a bit more about my job and learn a bit more about what an average day in the life of a junior data administrator at a meal delivery company looks like.

Elijah likes to talk, just like Russell did, but it's amazing how different he makes me feel when he does. I just want him to keep going. Elijah's humble and curious and excited about the world. Russell just bragged.

At one point, though, Elijah gets so lost in his own thoughts, he goes completely silent. For a few beats, he just stares into space. Not wanting to interfere, I stay quiet and wait for him to come back to the real world. There's something magical about getting to see him in such an intimate, uninhibited state. Eventually, when his glazed-over eyes slide over to me again, they instantly clear. He smiles, huge, like he's super relieved to still find me there sitting next to him. I can't resist beaming back.

"Can we go have sex now, please?" he says.

I choke on my coffee. Coughing, I release a stream of laughter. "Yes," I reply. "Yes, we can."

CHAPTER 10

"I really like this Elijah kid," I tell Kate on Monday as we walk to Bryant Park, our quinoa salads hovering in front of our chests. She's got me all to herself today. I have yet to even open any of the hookup apps. "Honestly," I continue, "I think I'd be happy just hanging out and hooking up with him until the baby comes."

"That sounds very boring and very unlike you," she replies, her big brown eyes scanning the famous skyscraper-ringed park. All the bistro tables are taken. She zones in on a young, suited-up Asian guy slouching in a chair by himself, a plastic bag full of what appears to be trash sitting on his table, stirring in the breeze. Marching up to him, she says, "Are you still using this table?"

His gaze lifts, he sees her, and he immediately gets up. She picks up his trash, passes it to him, and smacks her salad down on the table in its place. "Thanks," she says and sits down. I shuffle up to the table and plop into the other chair.

When we're alone, Cristian sometimes jokes that, for our next baby, Kate can be the surrogate and we can use my sperm instead of his. That way, Amelia can take a break and both of our kids can still have some color. The unlikelihood of that ever happening aside, I wouldn't be mad about it. Especially if the baby inherited Kate's chutzpah.

"By the way, which one's Elijah again?" she asks. "The producer?"

"No, the producer and I are over," I explain. "He, um, wanted more than I could give him. Elijah's the new twenty-two-year-old data boy I texted you about."

"The one from your Instagram story!"

I feel my cheeks warm. "That's the one." I don't usually put my fuckbuddies up on social media but Elijah was so goddamn adorable sucking on his iced latte on Saturday, I just couldn't resist. I snapped a photo and shared it with everyone I know.

"What a fuckin' cutie," Kate says.

"His personality's even cuter." The back of my neck grows hotter as I speak. "He's, like, the perfect guy. He's smart and polite and optimistic. He's got a great job. He's great in bed." I huff. "Seriously. I can't think of a single flaw."

"I can," Kate says. "He's a literal *baby*."

I tilt my head. "Come on, twenty-two's not *that* young."

She shrugs and lifts a forkful of quinoa to her mouth. For a moment, we eat in silence. I close my eyes, let the midday sun warm my eyelids.

Okay, maybe twenty-two *is* that young. But maybe that's a good thing. Being in Elijah's presence, even texting with him—and we've been doing a lot of texting since we saw each other—makes *me* feel younger. Is that a thing? Can youth be contagious? It's like he plunges me back into that sense of constant adventure and endless possibility I haven't really felt since I was a kid.

For the most part, my childhood was a good place. And so, for the most part, I don't mind revisiting it from time to time. White, middle class family. A brother who (mostly) had my back and vice versa. No deaths or tragedies. If you take out all the toxic moments of visceral homophobia that scarred me for life, you could even say it was damn near perfect. I could, however, have definitely done without that time I was eleven and watching a movie with my family in which a gay side character flirted with the male hero, and my dad, a bottle of beer in his hand, grunted, from right next to me on the sofa—so close I could smell the booze on his breath, "If I ever came across a faggot, I'd press him up against the wall and slit his throat."

Those words destroyed me. Especially since my father isn't—has never been—a violent man. He may overindulge in alcohol, sure, but he'd never hurt a fly, even when drunk off his ass. That day felt like a warning, aimed right at the center of my soul.

Then there was that time I was fifteen and my mom and I were at Walgreens and I asked her to buy me a tongue scraper because I was going through a period of paranoia about bad breath, and she whispered, in a lame attempt at a racy joke because I was a teenager now, "You don't need one. Those things are for homosexuals who want to get the taste of penis out of their mouths." She winked at me and finished with, "Just keep using your toothbrush on your tongue like a normal person."

I spent a lot of time thinking about that so-called joke of hers. It didn't make sense to me at all. So, what? Heterosexual women just went about with penis breath all day? And do penises, in themselves, being covered in nothing but human skin, even have a taste? But that type of thinking was only a self-imposed distraction. Because, the truth was, every time one of my parents or anyone else I was supposed to respect said such spiteful words, they killed a tiny part of me. A part I'll never get back. No wonder I'm a fucking pessimist with anxiety issues.

"You're not afraid of growing to like him a little too much?" Kate asks.

My eyes fly open. "What?"

"This Elijah kid."

I snort. "You're kidding, right?"

But Kate looks serious. "You're the one who said you'd be happy just hanging out and hooking up with him until the baby. What if you, like, develop feelings for him?"

I laugh. "We're just having fun. Hanging out with Elijah is refreshing. Easy. The producer guy drained so much out of me. I wasted way too much time on him."

"Has that ever happened before though?" she asks.

"What?"

"Have you ever had serious feelings for any of your boy toys?"

"No."

"So you never thought about leaving Cristian for any of them?"

"Of course not."

"Good," she says. "Because you know I love him."

My gaze drifts over to one of the other bistro tables, where a young mother is wiping smears of chocolate from her daughter's face.

There was a time, in the beginning, when Cristian and I first started dating, that I thought of him as a stand-in of sorts.

69

I'm not proud of it now, but we were young and he didn't tick off all the boxes I had in mind for my ideal long-term partner. Stupid, picky shit, like that his stomach wasn't flat enough or that he didn't make enough money. Just the usual, unrealistic expectations many of us have when we're tender-brained and delusional and think we're entitled to everything the world has to offer and more. I thought I'd be in a relationship with Cristian just until someone who ticked off more boxes came along. No one ever did. And, now, I'd never want anyone to.

"The guys I date," I say, "they're in a different category from Cristian. Cristian is…Cristian. No one can come close to what we have. Honestly, it just comes down to having complete faith in that. And I do."

"What about the other way around?" Kate asks. "Cristian dates other guys too. You've never been afraid that someone would steal him from you?"

"No one will," I say.

"But how can you know that?"

"I just know." I squint at her. "I can ask you the same thing, you know."

"What do you mean?"

"You're not afraid that Hiro will leave you for some cute girl in his office?" I love Kate's boyfriend, Hiro. He may not be the most brilliant straight boy out there but he's one of the most genuine and fun ones I've ever met. Whenever Kate brings him along to hang, it's a guaranteed good time.

"There are no cute girls in his office," she replies. "I checked."

I snort and drop the subject. I don't like explaining the inner workings of my relationship with Cristian, not even to Kate. It often feels like I'm either defending our choices or encouraging people to try open relationships for themselves. How can you put into words the intangible understanding you have with the man you love that what you offer him and what he offers you is and will be enough no matter what?

As for Cristian leaving me for someone else? You either love someone and you're loyal to them or you don't and you're not. Loyalty and monogamy are not mutually exclusive. Gay, straight, open, closed, it doesn't matter. Regardless of the circumstances, people are always at risk of falling victim to new love.

CHAPTER 11

Built over the remnants of the Domino Sugar Refinery and made into an urban playground, Domino Park on the Williamsburg waterfront is a sight to behold, especially on a warm, June Saturday when it's jam-packed with New York's finest. Young, beautiful faces smiling from behind expensive sunglasses. Young, beautiful bodies lounging on lawn chairs and chasing after volleyballs. Skin next to skin next to skin with the iconic Manhattan skyline just across the East River serving as the backdrop.

"Everything all right, mister?" Elijah asks, smiling up at me from the grass, his eyes slits against the midday sun. A zap of delight travels through me. I swear, every time Elijah smiles it's like he adds an extra year to my lifespan.

"Of course, cute stuff," I reply. "Just enjoying the view."

Running my gaze over his sprawled-out body, I take in his wide, naked chest and massive, bulging biceps. His arms lie in the grass above his head, next to his chic, neatly-folded shirt. The gray-brown bushes of his armpits are on full display.

We've already fucked today. After we did, he suggested we

grab lunch again and now we're at the park. Beyond a first date or two, which can serve as great build-up to sex, I'm never in public with my fuckbuddies. God, I can't even *imagine* doing this type of thing with someone like Ian. We'd run out of things to talk about in, like, ten minutes. But it's so easy to say yes to Elijah. And talking to him never feels like a chore.

I lower myself to the ground and once again line up my body next to his. Above us: bright blue sky.

"Do you have any siblings?" I ask.

"You've already asked me that."

There's a jolt of panic inside me. "I have?" I vaguely recall the moment but I'm unable to zone in on the details. "Oh, wait. Two sisters, right? One wants to be a pilot?"

Elijah snorts. "Nope. Wrong guy."

Embarrassed, because I probably *am* thinking of some other guy, I nudge his leg with mine. "Remind me, please."

"Just one brother. Younger. Wants to be a pharmacist."

"Oh, that's right!" I say, finally remembering. "Smart man. Where does he live?"

"Home, in Idaho."

A Shiba Inu swooshes past our heads, startling us both.

"Are you out to everybody in your family?" I ask after we settle back down.

"Yeah, pretty much."

"When did you come out?"

"Two years ago."

For a second, I'm confused, until I remember that Elijah's only twenty-two. Funny. The more I hang out with him the less conscious of the age difference I become. I guess when there's a connection, even a twelve-year gap ceases to matter. Still, with how comfortable Elijah is in his skin, I'm surprised it took him until twenty to come out. Not that there's a correct age or time to come out.

"How did it go?" I ask.

"It went okay, I guess. Especially considering the whole Mormon thing. But my parents have always been pretty liberal."

I lift my head and stare at him. "You're Mormon?" I ask. Had he told me that too and I forgot? No, I think that's something I'd remember.

"Not anymore," he answers. "But I was raised Mormon."

"I didn't know that..."

He chuckles. "I don't know your religious history, either."

"Good point." I drop my head back down to the grass. "Catholic," I say. "In case you're wondering."

"Did you go to Catholic school?"

"Sure did. Up until middle school."

"Did it scar you for life?"

Through a laugh, I say, "Of course. But it wasn't all bad. The first time I kissed a boy was in Catholic school, if you can believe it."

"Oh, I can," he says. "Best friend or star athlete?"

"Neither. Some transfer kid."

"Do tell."

"Not much to tell. One time, in math, I had to pee, so I got a hall pass. He was in the bathroom when I got there. I didn't even know his name. We were both at the sink, washing our hands. There was something about the way he was looking at me. I don't know how I got the courage—we'd never exchanged a single word before that day—but I dried my hands and straight up asked him if he wanted to kiss me."

74

"Whoa," Elijah says. "That's very outgoing of you. And adorable."

"It kind of is, no?" I say, suddenly warmed by the fond memory.

"You probably made that kid's day. Did you guys start dating after that?"

I laugh. "No, it was just that one time."

"When did you come out?" Elijah asks.

"When I was your age, actually. Twenty-two."

"How did it go for you?"

"No so well," I reply with a sigh, slightly distracted by a shirtless jogger's gleaming, perfectly sculpted torso.

In the grass between us, Elijah's hand lands on mine. "We don't have to talk about it if you don't want to," he says.

"Oh, no no. I don't mind." I puff out my cheeks. "It's not that interesting anyway. Just lots of shame and self-loathing. You know, typical Catholic stuff."

"Is your family super religious?"

"I wouldn't say *that*… But they do go to church every Sunday. And, I mean, I don't blame my parents for being brought up to believe homosexuality is, like, the greatest—not to mention the most revolting—sin of all time or whatever. Or for the way they reacted when I first told them. But I do—well, I did, anyway—blame them for taking so long to come around."

"How long are we talking?"

"The better part of my twenties."

"Oof…"

"Yeah…they refused to acknowledge it, even though I was living openly. Being away from them, in Spain, helped."

I think about all the toxic words my parents forced me to listen to throughout the years while I was still in the closet. Those words weren't meant to intentionally hurt me, and I doubt my parents would even remember any of them today, but I do. I remember them all. Every single one. But that was the thing. In the end, thankfully, words is the furthest they took it. When he found about me, my father never actually pushed me up against the wall and slit my throat like he'd claimed he would if he ever came across a faggot. Some gay kids aren't as lucky.

Not to diminish the power of words. Words can be weapons. Maybe that's why languages fascinate me so much. Why I became a translator. The more languages and words you know, the more weapons you have at your disposal. The more weapons, the more ways to protect yourself.

"Me being gay didn't exactly fit with the plan they had envisioned for me," I go on. "Which is actually what pissed me off the most in the end. Because they made my coming out about themselves, you know? Like it was the worst thing that's ever happened to *them*. My mom even used it as an excuse to start drinking again, even though she was sober for five years at that point. Said I drove her back to it."

Elijah winces. "I'm sorry to hear that..."

"It's fine. She stopped again a few years ago. Not my dad, though." I snort. "His drinking problem is pretty permanent. Anyway, it took a while, but both my parents did come around eventually. Now they're pretty ashamed of how they handled the whole thing. To the point that my brother thinks they love me more than they love him."

"Ha. He told you that?"

"Yeah, we got high one night and he poured his heart out. And I was like: 'Good, they *should* love me more because there was a time when they didn't at all.'"

76

Elijah squeezes my hand. "I'm sure they still did. Even when it seemed like they didn't."

Again, I lift my head up from the grass, but, this time, I give him a kiss. One of those long, lazy ones, where your lips stay connected for a while, with little movement, as if you're recharging each other's batteries. Pulling away, I say, "Okay, let's talk about something a little less depressing. Tell me about your first sexy time with a dude."

He snorts. "It doesn't get any more depressing than that."

"What? Why?"

His face contorts, as if the memory actually causes him physical pain.

"*That* bad?" I ask.

He sucks in a deep breath. "It was just…ugh. I didn't enjoy a single second of it. I thought I might actually be asexual or something. I already knew I wasn't into girls and that experience made me think guys weren't for me either…"

"When was this?"

"Not long after I came out."

"So within the last two years?"

"Yes."

I lay my head back down. "You do enjoy sex with *me*, though, right? Because it sure seems to me like you do."

Elijah laughs, prodding me with his shoulder. "Yes," he says. Then, more quietly but also more seriously, he adds, "A lot, actually."

A bubble of pride swells within me. "But so what made it so bad that first time? Was the guy really gross or something? Who was it?"

"Just a random guy from campus. He wasn't bad looking or

anything…. I just wasn't attracted to him for some reason. But, I don't know…I was already in his dorm room, and I *was* a little curious, I guess, so I just went along with it."

"Okay, that sounds like *exactly* what I wanted to avoid with my first time."

"Oh yeah? Tell me about yours."

"Mine was great. I got what I paid for."

Elijah props himself up on his elbow. "No way. You paid for a prostitute?"

"*Escort*," I enunciate.

He laughs. "How old were you?"

"Twenty."

"Was he hot?"

"Oh yeah," I say. "Even better looking in person than in his photos. That was the whole point. To choose a guy I was one hundred percent attracted to."

"What was he like?"

"Hungarian," I say as I remember climbing the three flights of stairs to the man's apartment. Knocking on his door, my young heart banging, my ears hot. "His name was Zsolt. Twenty-nine, hairy chest, legs, arms. Just all around *man*, you know?"

Elijah chuckles. "Oh I *know*. Sounds hot."

"He was sweet, too. Before we got started, he was like, 'Are you sure you want to do this?' Then he explained to me that I shouldn't have to pay for sex because I'm good looking. He suggested I go to a bar instead where someone would scoop me up."

"Aw," Elijah says. "That *is* sweet. Not very good for business though."

"I know… I told him: 'No, it's okay, I know what I'm doing.' And then we did it and it was perfect. I wanted to be in control and that's exactly what happened. Money well spent. Honestly, I'd recommend the experience to anybody."

"Did you top? Bottom?"

"Neither. We mostly did hand stuff. I sucked his dick for a bit. I was too scared of STDs to do more. You know, escort and all that."

"Have you ever had an STD?" Elijah asks.

My neck grows even warmer than it already is from the sun. But, for some reason, I feel the urge to be completely honest with him. "Yeah," I answer. "Chlamydia. Twice. It's really common though," I add quickly. "You just pop a pill and it's gone."

Elijah chuckles. "Don't worry. I'm not judging."

"You?"

"Not yet," he says. "Maybe you can give me one."

"Okay, I'll try," I say with a wink. "Just keep having tons of sex with me."

Before we know it, the sun has made it to the other side of the East River. I sit up. On the esplanade, tourists line the fence, taking photos with the Empire State Building in the background. I check the time on my phone. Cristian will be getting out of work soon. I promised to be waiting for him outside of his studio when he does. We're supposed to pop by a few stores to look at baby clothes before heading home.

Elijah too pulls himself up into a sitting position. "Is our time up already, Mister Married Man?" he asks.

"Unfortunately," I say, quietly wishing that it wasn't.

CHAPTER 12

The following Saturday, Elijah invites me to hang with him again. If I could, I'd readily agree. Alas, I'm unable to see him because I'm taking Amelia to the zoo.

Yes, the fucking zoo.

Do you want to grab coffee with me Saturday? I texted her two days prior, after yet another not-so-gentle nudge from Cristian.

No, she replied. *But I do want to see snow leopards.*

At least she's not making us trek all the way to the Bronx and the zoo there. That would be a whole-day endeavor. Although, if she were going there, I doubt she'd have invited me along. I bet she wants to spend as little time with me as I do with her. The much closer and much smaller zoo in Central Park, we can both do.

Walking into the huge foyer of her ten-story building, I smile at the middle-aged concierge sitting behind the front desk. Amelia lives on the Upper East Side. Not because she's rich herself but because she's "taking care of" an apartment that belongs to her rich ninety-year-old aunt. It's highly unlikely that the aunt will ever make it across the Atlantic Ocean again. Let's just say Amelia lucked out big-time.

The concierge eyes me like he's unsure whether he knows me or not, which makes sense because I'm not here very often and, when I am, I'm always with Cristian. "Amelia in 8D," I say. Recognition flickers in his eye and he gestures for me to proceed.

In the elevator, I get a text from Elijah.

Hello, mister, it says.

Hi, cute stuff, I reply. *What are you up to?*

Just planning my trip to Brazil. And you?

Just got to Amelia's. Elijah knows who Amelia is and what she's doing for Cristian and me. He also knows how much I'm looking forward to my zoo trip with her.

Smiling face emoji. *Good luck! I miss you.*

I miss you too, I write back.

What Elijah doesn't know yet, however, is that, come September, if I'm still seeing him, I'll have to stop. And, with how things are going and how much fun I'm having, I'm pretty sure I'll want to keep hanging out with him for as long as I can. So I'll have to tell him about the deadline. I just need to find the right moment.

When the biological mother of my future daughter opens the door to her apartment there's a curt smile on her face. "Greg," she says.

"Amelia," I reply.

Her eyes veer to the big paper bag in my hand, which contains a knitting kit, a how-to guide, and a bunch of colorful yarn. Cristian made me get all this before I got here because Amelia let it be known that she needs a creative outlet that's not work-related. I bet you she'll pick this shit up once for, like, five minutes and never touch it again. "You can just leave that on the kitchen counter," she tells me. "Thanks."

Like I mentioned, Amelia is a freelance graphic designer. I've never actually seen anything she's done, but, allegedly, she's worked for some big-name clients. According to her own policy, though, she only takes on work that aligns with her values. Which, to me, basically means that she doesn't take on a lot of work. But then again, she's got her aunt's apartment. In New York, as long as your rent is covered, you're set.

As usual, when I'm here, my gaze wafts over to the back wall in the living room, to the stunning painting of a topless Amelia smoking a cigarette. It's based on a Polaroid photo her ex-husband took during a trip to Mallorca that a bunch of us went on some eight or nine years ago. I've always been secretly salty about the fact that Cristian has painted a portrait of her and has yet to do mine.

While Amelia slips on her loafers, I realize how nervous I am. Much more so than I would be with a random guy I met on one of the apps. It feels like there's so much more at stake here. This is the mother of my future child. In the eleven years that I've known her, we've managed to tolerate one another, but that's because we were only really alone together in moments when Cristian would leave to go to the bathroom or when the two of us would arrive somewhere before he did.

"So why the zoo?" I ask on the elevator ride down.

"Why not?" she responds.

Whether I want it or not, Amelia's going to be a huge part of the rest of my life. What I say and do today will affect the future course of our relationship. What if today's bonding session, instead of bringing us closer, tears us further apart?

"Do you want me to call a car?" I ask once we get to the foyer.

"No," she says. "We're walking."

"Are you sure?" I ask, surprised. "It's pretty hot out. And that's a good ten blocks down. Should you be doing that much walking?"

The second the question leaves my mouth, I regret asking it. The flicker of annoyance on Amelia's face only confirms that I should.

"Sorry," I say.

Out of freaking nowhere, Amelia stops and both her arms bolt up above her head. She bounces herself back and launches a perfectly straightened leg forward. Three times, it goes flying up in the air in an impressive display of three consecutive cheerleading jump kicks. I'm so stunned, all I can do is stand there like "what the fuck just happened" while the concierge's clapping and laughter echo through the lobby.

Amelia does a little bow and winks at him before she turns to me. "If I can do this, I can go for a little walk, don't you think?"

I nod. "Is cheerleading even a thing in the UK?" I ask.

"Not really. But I've been trying to make it a thing there since I was twelve."

I fight back a smile. Sometimes, I'll get glimpses of why Cristian loves this girl so much. Hopefully, after today, the future will only bring more.

Amelia prowls the streets of the Upper East Side like a lioness looking after her territory. For a few blocks, we walk down Madison Avenue, past the numerous upscale fashion boutiques lining it. Seeing her eye a few items on display in the windows,

I half expect her to come to the conclusion that one of the more expensive summer dresses would somehow be great for the baby. To my relief, however, she doesn't. She turns right and leads us west, toward Fifth Avenue. Once we reach it, we make our way south, down the length of Central Park's eastern side, toward the zoo.

The green wall of trees to our right and the white facades of luxury apartment buildings to our left, we pass hot dog stands and the Manhattan-enamored tourists lining up to buy their overpriced wieners. We watch the local wealthy older ladies in coats—always in coats—ambling up to their taxis accompanied by their doormen. The walk is a pleasant one, even if Amelia and I are silent throughout most of it. When we do talk, inevitably, all topics lead back to Cristian and babies.

At the zoo, I pay for our tickets and let her lead the way. "Let's see the sea lions first," she says. I nod and follow a step behind.

While we watch the funny-looking, whiskery animals bob their heads in and out of the water, little kids giggling in delight all around us, I catch a small smile on Amelia's lips. It looks peaceful and sincere. Non-threatening, for a change.

"So what is it?" I ask in a gentle tone. "Why have you never liked me?"

Amelia sighs, but her smile remains intact. "It's not that I don't like you, Greg," she says. "It's that Cristian is the biggest sweetheart in the world."

I nod. Matter-of-factly, I say, "You don't think I'm good enough for him."

"Honestly, it doesn't matter what I think because, clearly, he's in love with you and he's very happy. I want us to be better friends, too, you know. For Cristian's sake. And for the baby's, obviously."

"But what is it exactly that makes you question my love for him? What did I do?"

"That thing where you forced an open marriage on him, for one."

I whip my face her way and scoff. "I did no such thing. *He* brought it up. Then we discussed it and we both agreed that opening up would be best for us."

"Would be best for *you*," she says like she's correcting me. "If it was up to Cristian, you wouldn't be open. He did it for you, Greg. You took advantage of his generosity and you know it."

My face is burning. I knew Amelia didn't pull any punches, but this is a more painful beating than I saw coming. I want to point out that Cristian has never exactly been hesitant about seeing other guys either, but I don't. I also *really* want to give her my two cents as to who it is exactly who's taking advantage of Cristian's generosity, but I want to avert a disaster, so I keep that to myself as well.

"It's fine," she goes on. "Again, it's your life and it's Cristian's. For some reason, Cristian is happy with you and that's all that matters. That's why I offered to have your baby. Honesty, I thought you wouldn't even want one. You don't seem like the type who'd want to be changing diapers all day."

So that's how she sees me. "Are you disappointed that I agreed?" I ask.

"No," she replies. "Quite the opposite."

I scratch my chin. "Look," I say. "I made the decision to have a baby with the man I love. I don't really care how other people feel about that. Not even you."

"And you shouldn't," she says. "You asked so I'm telling you."

In silence, she turns and begins strolling towards the next exhibit. I follow. "For your information," I tell her, "we're closing up again."

"I heard," she says. "I think it's a good idea."

Of course she does. No surprises there. The thought that closing up might have been a prerequisite of hers for carrying our baby crosses my mind, but that's unlikely to be the case. When she invited us to that dinner and made the offer to be our surrogate, Cristian was just as astonished as I was.

"I don't like the fact that your Spanish is better than mine, either," she says.

"Huh?" I ask.

"Another reason I never liked you." She looks at me, grinning.

I stretch my lips into a smile. "Okay. Now *this* I understand."

Indoors, in the Tropic Zone, while black-and-white lemurs lick their crotches in their fake little jungle settings, I ask, "How's *your* love life?"

"Not much of a love life at the moment," she replies. "But I do have my ex Daniel come over to eat me out two or three times a week. He's really into the pregnant thing."

"Oh..."

"Again," she says, "you asked."

When Amelia goes to the bathroom, I discover, on my phone, two missed calls from someone I never expected to hear from again: Russell Mailey. Seeing the name on my screen makes me frown with dread. What the hell does he want?

With my thumb, I tap his name. The phone starts dialing.

A crackle. Then, on the other end, I hear: "Hi."

"Hi," I say, warily. "What's up, Russell."

"You called me back."

"I did. What's up?"

"How are you?"

I feel a bite of annoyance. "Good. What can I do for you?"

He takes a long breath. "Listen. I thought about it and you were right. I did talk about myself a lot. I can see now how I might've come off as a bit narcissistic."

"Aha..."

"The truth is, I was just trying to impress you," he goes on. "I wanted you to like me, and, I guess, I got carried away. Sorry about that."

"Um. It's fine, don't worry about it."

"And...I thought...maybe, you'd want to meet up."

"Why?"

"Try this again."

For a beat, I hold my breath. "No thanks," I say, releasing it.

Silence. The breeze carries over the particularly zoo-like stink of shit and piss.

"I have to stop seeing other men soon," I add, because I feel a little bad. "My husband and I are closing up when the baby comes. Sorry."

Russell's breathing grows heavier, more erratic. "I see..."

"Yeah..."

A long pause. Then: "You really would do anything for some dick, wouldn't you, Greg?"

Even though I'm sweating, I feel a chill. Those words. I've heard them before. No. I've *read* them before. On the screen of my phone. Scared and surrounded by darkness and empty warehouses.

My breathing intensifies. "Was that you?" I ask. "A few weeks ago? On Grindr? Did you catfish me, Russell?"

"You really need to do some work on yourself."

I grit my teeth. "It *was* you, wasn't it?"

"Especially if you're going to be a father."

Just as I'm about to tell him what a piece of shit he is, how sick and fucked up of a thing that was of him to do, the call ends. "Hello?" I try, just to make sure. "Russell?" But all I hear on the other end is silence. He hung up.

Angry and frustrated, I stand there, my mind reeling. The catfishing incident happened before Russell and I started seeing each other. But he did find me on Grindr that time I spent my last evening with my regular, Ian. Is it possible that Russell had already been stalking me on there before we've even met? What a fucking creep. And why would he catfish me in the first place? Was it some kind of sick test? I don't know what the bastard meant to accomplish by scaring me like that, but I do know, all the way in the depths of my being, without a grain of doubt, that it was him.

"What's wrong?" Amelia's voice asks, startling me. She's back from the bathroom, eyeing me with skepticism. "You look like you've seen a ghost."

I clear my throat and manufacture a chuckle. "I kind of have."

"Okay...Are you ready?" she asks.

"For what?"

She cocks an eyebrow. "For the snow leopards, stupid. What else?"

CHAPTER 13

Outside of that unwelcome phone call from fuck-face Russell, my bonding session with Amelia was a success. Cristian was pleased.

I make up for not being able to hang out with Elijah over the weekend by swinging over to his place the night before he leaves for Brazil and giving him an extra good bon voyage-style dick-down because I won't see him again for a while. Afterwards, we take edibles and watch reality TV. I get home at 2 a.m.

Saturday, on my day to myself, I return to my regularly scheduled whoring around. I haven't hooked up with anyone besides Elijah in a while.

My first opportunity comes in the form of a young, WASPy tennis player I had briefly chatted with two or three weeks prior, promised to hang with at some point in the future, and then completely forgot about. He hits me up on Grindr as soon as I open it in the morning, which is five minutes after Cristian kisses me goodbye and leaves for work.

Hey, the tennis player says.

Hey, I reply to the tennis player.

Looking?

The reason I'm referring to the tennis player as "the tennis player" is because he has a tennis ball emoji in his profile. For all I know, he doesn't even play tennis.

Scrolling up, I reevaluate the two photos he'd sent me the last time we chatted and immediately remember why I hadn't been too eager to follow up with him. I had yet to make an official decision on whether I was actually attracted to him or not.

Let me see some more of you, I ask and follow my request with three photos of myself that he hasn't yet seen. I send one of me in Red Hook holding a lobster roll. One of me in front of an Adidas store mirror, trying to look broody. And one of me shirtless from last summer getting ready to jump into a swimming hole up in the Adirondacks.

He instantly responds with three photos of his own.

If Grindr photos were currency, face pics would be ten-dollar bills, shirtless pics twenties, faceless nudes fifties, and, nudes-with-face, hundreds. In this case, I get a ten and two fifties. The ten has his round, boyish face in it. His run-of-the-mill, circumcised penis takes center stage in the two fifties.

He's a little twinkier than what I'd usually go for but he does have an appealing treasure trail on his flat stomach and I'm kind of digging the big bush it's connected to. I think I want to see it in person.

Cute, I reply. *My place in an hour?*

Sure! Address?

After I shower, I make an egg-and-cheese sandwich and pour myself a cup of coffee. Then I sit in front of my laptop and put on some porn to warm myself up. I believe one should always stretch before a workout.

As I'm stretching, I get another *Looking?* message on Grindr from another boy I'd chatted with a few weeks back—a lean French guy with a dreamy, boy-band haircut. Instantly, I sit up because, this boy, I didn't forget about. This boy, I remember very well.

Hey, I reply as fast as my thumb allows. *Yeah I am.*

He types back: *Would you like to come over?*

Yeah, I say. *When?*

In an hour?

Fuck. *What about in two?* I ask. Heart pounding, I wait for a response.

I don't think I can host then, he says. My stomach starts to sink but then he adds, *Can you?*

YES!

Great.

Maybe I can even do an hour and a half. I'll keep you posted.

Chugging the rest of my coffee, I dash to the bathroom and rip open a new enema box. Both of these dudes claim to be versatile so I need to be prepared. If I were still in my twenties, I'd have no problem cumming with both of them as well. Unfortunately, I'm no longer in my twenties. The plan is to warm-up with the tennis player and then have my finale with the Frenchie. The tennis player is twenty-three. I bet I can make him cum at the snap—or stroke, in this case—of my fingers.

When my phone pings with a *Here* from the tennis player, I still have my toothbrush in my mouth. *One sec*, I text and spit into the sink.

The tennis player looks pretty much exactly like he did in his photos. Meek, boyish, on the slim side. Unfortunately, his photos didn't convey anything about his penchant for hideous leather jackets with fringes. And why is he even wearing a jacket? It's literally eighty degrees out.

"Hi," I say with a tight smile.

"Hi," he replies and sneaks inside.

As I'm flipping the lock on my door, I realize how nervous he is. "Thanks for coming," I say, hoping to break some of the ice.

"Thank you for having me," he replies. In a shaky voice, he adds, "You're really, *really* attractive."

"Thanks. Back at you!" I say, even though I don't actually think so. He's cute and polite and all but he doesn't hold a candle to Cristian …or Elijah. I'd offer him a coffee, that's what I usually do when I invite a guy over, but I'm on a tight schedule.

His rather conspicuous Adam's apple jumps. "So what do you think?" he asks, the question universal gay code for: "so do you still want to hook up?"

Even though I can still apologize and send him home—which I probably should do since, to be completely honest, I'm still on the fence about whether I'm actually attracted to him or not—I don't have the heart to say no.

"I'm good," I reply. "You?"

The words "me too" fly out of his mouth and, a second later, he's pressing his lips to mine. He's rough and awkward, unable to control his lust. Cristian is not only a painter. He's also an artist with his kisses. This kid is digging a ditch.

I let him give me some uninspired head, but five minutes in, I'm over it. Reaching down, I pull him up by his armpits and jostle him over to my bedroom, where I sit him down on the bed and start undoing his jeans.

"You're going to make me cum," he whimpers less than a minute later. He tries to shield his cock with his hand but I smack the hand away.

I wouldn't consider myself a grade-A cocksucker but I've gotten better over the years. I'd say I'm a solid B. Although, I'm pretty sure even an E for effort would be enough to make this inexperienced youngling writhe with ecstasy.

At the last second, I disengage my mouth and watch him squirt onto his happy trail. Patting his thigh, I stand up and grab a towel. "I have to leave soon," I say. "Lunch plans. But thanks for coming." I throw in a wink.

"What about you?" he asks, indicating my now completely flaccid cock. He sounds like he's on the verge of crying.

"I'm okay for today," I say. "You can make me cum next time."

The words "next time" extract somewhat of a smile out of him. Still, the silent minute while he puts on his shoes is physically excruciating. I grind my teeth together and will him to move faster. I think about asking him about tennis, but that might get a whole new conversation going and the hot Frenchie is waiting.

"This was great," I lie after he stands before me, his fringed jacket once again hanging from his skinny frame.

"I'd love to see you again sometime," he says.

"For sure." I smile and unlock my door.

"I never got your name."

"Greg."

"Nice to meet you Greg. I'm Preston."

"Likewise, Preston."

"Can I have your number?"

"Um," I say, "I'll send it to you on the app." He nods and walks through the threshold. "Take care."

As soon as I shut the door behind him, my phone is back in my hand and I'm typing up a message to the French guy. He comes over about twenty minutes later.

Opportunity Number Two makes a much more positive first impression. He radiates swagger and he's wearing a T-shirt without any jacket over it.

This guy, I do offer a coffee. He asks for water. We sit on my couch and I begin to interrogate him with the usual questions. This is what I find out:

His name is Guillame, he's twenty-nine, he works as a butler-adjacent something or other for a wealthy Saudi family living in France and he has accompanied the head of that family to New York on business. He's kind of boring but I could watch him rake his boy-band hair with his long fingers as he scours his brain for English words all day.

"So you're staying in Brooklyn?" I ask.

"No. Upper West Side. But my school friend from my youth lives close to your home," he explains, which must be why I haven't seen him on my neighborhood Grindr since that first time we chatted a few weeks back.

"I'm glad you hit me up again," I say with what I'm hoping is a sexy grin. I guess it has the intended effect because a minute later I have his small-headed but thick-based, uncut eggplant of a cock in my mouth. After a while, with his adventurous fingers, he makes it clear that he wants to fuck more than my face.

While I'm under him, my legs wrapped around his lower half, his hot breath filling the inch of space between our faces as he thrusts, a random, but very distracting image of Elijah also being pinned down to a bed—but not by me, by some hung Brazilian guy—enters my mind.

I'm trying to refocus on the task at hand, when, all of a sudden, Guillame stiffens up and all of his weight falls on top of me.

After a moment, crushed by his unmoving bulk, I say, "Um. Did you cum?"

"Oui," he grunts into the side of my neck.

"Oh…"

His size expands as he takes a big breath, pushing me deeper into the bed. Then he lifts himself off me and starts peeling off the condom.

His eyes flick up. "Do you want to cum?"

Of course I want to cum. But after the apathetic way he asks, I think I'll pass. "No. It's okay," I say. "It felt really good, though." I hand him the same towel I handed the tennis player earlier and he leaves soon after.

At this point, I'm kind of hungry. I grab a packet of smoked salmon from the fridge and cut open an avocado. The food fails to quench my horniness, however, and so as soon as I'm done eating I'm back on Grindr. Fifteen minutes after that, I'm in an Uber heading down to Bed-Stuy to meet some fit Asian dude and his considerably less fit white boyfriend. Hopefully, the third time's the charm.

The fit Asian dude opens the door in nothing but white Calvin Klein briefs. His name is Aaron and he's missing a tooth. Not a front one, but you can still see the gap when he smiles. The considerably less fit white guy sits on a big sofa chair in an open bathrobe, stroking his stumpy penis. I beeline towards him.

After I finally get my orgasm, I feel kind of gross. And, honestly, kind of ashamed. Who does this? Three hookups in a row only to get off during an underwhelming threesome? I should've just jerked off and called it a day.

I'm starting to panic. That's what this is. I'm trying to hoard as many hookups as possible because my mind is involuntarily equating my impending monogamy with the goddamn apocalypse. Which is fucking ridiculous. As usual, I'm overthinking and overdoing. I'm fucking for the sake of fucking and I don't like it.

I bid the couple farewell and get on the bus home. I shower and head over to Williamsburg to wait for Cristian so we can get groceries and have a quiet night in.

When my husband sees me outside his studio, he gives me his huge, Mediterranean smile. He's changed from his work coveralls into a white pocket T-shirt and a pair of loose-fitting Levi's, but I can still spot some paint stains on the underside of his forearm. He probably missed them while washing up.

"Hi, mi amor," he says and, within me, everything aligns. And, even though it's already 6 p.m., I feel like this is when my day finally begins.

CHAPTER 14

It was a dry, hot night in late October, I remember that much, although I always forget the exact date. I was out on the town in Chueca, the main gay district in Madrid, still riding the high of having recently moved to a foreign country and scoring my first real translator gig. A few friends I had met in that very same gay district only a couple of weeks prior accompanied me that night, but, after my eyes found him, I couldn't tell you what those friends did or how long they stayed.

What drew me to Cristian wasn't his height or facial scruff, although I'm sure those factors played a part. Of all things, the initial magnet was the baseball cap on his head. I know. I was the basic, fresh-out-of-college, masc-for-masc baby gay drawn to a baseball cap like a moth to a flame. Don't blame me. Blame the type of masculinity I grew up with. Anyway, when I first spotted him in the crowd, squeezed in by a bunch of lanky boys in bright-colored tank tops, I thought: now *that's* a man.

As soon as the friend he was with—a chubby guy named Lilo, who I'd grow to love like a brother—left for the bathroom, I made my move. Sometimes, I still wonder how things would've played out if Amelia had been there with them that night.

Until I weaved past all the sweaty bodies and spoke to him, I had assumed Cristian didn't know I existed. Since I first spotted him, I kept undressing him with my eyes, but he didn't even glance at me once. "Hi," I said, nervous. "I'm Greg."

Under his bushy eyebrows, his brown eyes widened in surprise. At the time, I thought it was because I was American and speaking English, but he later told me it was actually because he was, indeed, very much aware of my existence. He just didn't bother eye-fucking me because he'd assumed I was out of his league.

"Cristian," he replied in that deep but sweet voice of his. Feeling his strong grip around my hand and seeing the corners of his eyes crinkle from his beautiful smile, I made the decision to try anything to get him in bed. What I didn't know was just how long this goal would take to achieve. Five months, to be exact. The reason? At the time of our meeting in that sweaty club on that hot October night, my dear Cristian was in a serious, monogamous relationship with someone else.

Still, I kept Cristian in my orbit, inviting him out to eat and drink, both when I was alone and when I was with friends. I accepted every single invitation to hang out with him and his friends, including Amelia, whom I'd sometimes catch observing me with a tinge of prudence from where she clung to her then-husband's arm.

Cristian's boyfriend, an older university professor he had been dating for about a year at that point, never joined us. I met him in person, in passing, only once but I knew a lot about the guy from Cristian's stories.

"He didn't invite you along?" I asked Cristian one night as

the two of us sat on a Chueca curb at 4 a.m., kebabs hovering in front of our hungry mouths. His boyfriend had left him alone for the weekend and jetted off to Ibiza with someone else.

"No," Cristian replied.

"Do you know *who* he went with?"

A shrug. "Someone he knows from the university."

There was no need to point out that "someone he knows from the university" probably meant: "a twenty-year-old male student he's fucking on the side". Cristian was well aware of what his boyfriend was up to. He might be a little too trusting sometimes but he's never been stupid. I didn't want to be a dick and rub it in. Secretly, though, I was, of course, happy. What this meant was that his relationship already had cracks in it. All it needed was a few more taps and it would shatter completely.

Not only was Cristian really good-looking—I could not get over his eyebrows and big, manly hands—he was a talented artist with a unique point of view. I was obsessed. I thought about him all day. I dreamt about him all night. I yearned to be the subject of his loyalty instead of that undeserving tool of an old fart he was with. Waiting for Cristian to respond to my texts was almost a physical pain.

My mind returns to the present and I look down at my phone.

"Elijah?" Cristian calls over from the fitting room, where he's trying on a suit for my cousin's upcoming wedding in California.

Heat blazes my cheeks. I yank my eyes away from the screen and slip my phone back in my pocket. My husband is peeking at me from behind the fitting room curtain. The suit that, just moments ago, was on a hanger is now on his body. Clearing my throat, I put on a big smile and say, "Looks great! I think this might be the one."

Cristian pushes the curtain all the way open and starts studying himself in the mirror. He does this with as much intensity in his eyes and facial muscles as he does while painting. The simple, clean suit is an elegant complement to his rugged looks. He'll definitely be stealing the show, as usual.

Pride fills my chest. Eleven years I have been with this man. *Eleven years.* That's practically a third of my life.

Cristian was half right: just now, Elijah didn't text me, but I was checking my phone in the hope that he did. I haven't seen him since he got back from Brazil and it's been hours since I asked if he's free tomorrow night.

Cristian knows who Elijah is because I can't seem to keep Elijah's name out of my damn mouth. Most recently, I brought him up while Cristian and I were watching a Netflix show in bed and a bunch of Mormons came on. "Oh! Elijah actually grew up Mormon. Did I tell you that?" Like I said, I like sharing my experiences with Cristian, whether he wants me to or not.

"Okay, this one will do," Cristian announces, beaming at me. I beam back and nod approvingly. Good timing, too, because the store is about to close.

The night I finally got to sleep with my future husband is etched in my mind in perfect detail, even if I don't remember the exact date. Before it happened, I had already extended numerous invitations for him to come back to my place after a dinner in Malasaña or a night out in Chueca. I was always playful about it, made it sound like a joke. No doubt Cristian was well aware of how I felt about him and what my intentions were, but I didn't want to come off as too sleazy and Cristian had a boyfriend. I was also much younger then. I didn't have the confidence I have now.

We had just finished eating burgers at a new American joint neither of us had been to before. Cristian hadn't trimmed his facial hair in a while. He was looking extra scruffy and scrumptious. "Should we go get some beer now?" he asked, slouching back in his chair, his hand patting his satisfied belly.

"I have beer at my place," I said, bouncing my eyebrows.

Cristian's expression didn't waver. "Okay."

For a couple of beats, I was so paralyzed I couldn't speak. So I just sat there, staring at him. Cristian stayed silent too, staring back. We kept looking into each other's eyes, communication so many things at once. After all this time, after so many polite brush-offs, Cristian had finally agreed to come over.

The train ride home that night? The anticipation of what was about to come? God, it was electric. I was rock hard just from thinking about it. Every time the skin of our elbows grazed, I nearly ejaculated. Not joking. To this day, that night with Cristian and everything leading up to it remains one of the most thrilling experiences of my life.

To my enormous delight, that first time, Cristian spent the night. The next morning, holding the bagel I toasted for him in one hand, he plucked his phone out of his fallen jeans and, right there on the spot, broke up with his toxic professor boyfriend. "I cheated on him," he told me after he hung up. "It was the right thing to do."

I was the happiest boy in Spain.

Today, riding the train home with Cristian has its own pleasures. The days of sizzling electricity between us are long gone, but that's okay. The sparks have been replaced with safety, comfort, reassurance. I'm intimately acquainted with everything about him. I know the intricacies of his face, the imperfections of his body. His voice and the words he utters with it. All of those things correlate to my comprehension of love.

On reflex, I check my phone. My heart speeds up when I see a new text, but I get a sting of disappointment when I realize it's not a reply from Elijah but a video meme from Kate. I let it play. A wobbling baby trips and falls flat onto its round, puffy face. I angle the screen towards Cristian and we chuckle together.

"We're not letting Kate anywhere near our daughter," he says.

"Agreed," I reply.

The train reaches Essex/Delancey. The two middle-aged Asian ladies we've been looming over get up from their seats. Cristian and I take their places.

"Oh," Cristian says. "Remember Jared?"

"Yeah. From your studio, right?"

"Yes," Cristian replies. "His aunt has done some nanny work in the past. He says she's super sweet. He can introduce us whenever."

"Oh nice. I'd much rather do that than interview total strangers."

"Exactly. Also, don't forget about Amelia's doctor's appointment on Tuesday."

"I won't."

New bodies fill up the train to replace the ones that got off. Three of them belong to athletic-looking young men, one of them shirtless, his dark brown skin snugly stretched over his muscles. From experience, I already know they're performers who intend to use the longer stretch between Manhattan and

Brooklyn to collect some tips. As expected, blaring music fills the car and they launch into their handrail acrobatics. Some people's eyes roll in annoyance. Others' light up with excitement.

I bump Cristian's arm with my own. He turns to me and I mouth the words, "Te quiero." He smiles and does the same.

In Bushwick, we get off at Knickerbocker and grab takeout from our favorite Mexican place. Once we get home, I hang our new suits in the closet while Cristian goes to the bathroom to remove his contacts. I'm about to unpack our food when I glance at my phone one final time for the night.

And there, on my screen, I see Elijah's name.

A small, silent bomb of relief detonates within me. He finally texted me back. Upon closer inspection, I see that he's sent me four texts in a row, which is unusual, but I tell myself not to read them. Not tonight. Tonight is all about Cristian. Elijah made me wait. I can do the same to him. But even as I'm thinking this, I already know I won't be able to resist.

And so I read them. And then I read them again. By the time I read the texts for the third time, my heart is pounding. This is what Elijah wrote:

Text one: *I'm so sorry! Been dealing with some work crap.*

Text two: *I miss you, mister. I really want to see you.*

Text three: *Can I? Tonight? Just for a little bit. I have something for you.*

Text four: *Please.*

From what feels like a great distance, I register the sound of running water in the bathroom. I can't possibly see Elijah tonight. Does he expect me to just come running anytime it's convenient for him? I'm a married man.

But Elijah's words, especially the "miss you" and "please" parts keep echoing through mind. And, just like I knew I wouldn't be able to resist reading his texts, I know I won't be able to resist his request to see me.

Chapter 15

"He wanted to give me a souvenir," I tell Kate at lunch the next day when I'm recounting the previous night's events. "And to have sex, obviously."

"Aww," she replies, her mouth opening wide enough for me a to see the crushed remnants of her veggie burrito on her tongue. "What was the souvenir?"

"A pair of boxer shorts with a giant anteater on them."

Kate's nose wrinkles. "Are anteaters a Brazilian thing?"

"I guess? Ask your Japanese-Brazilian man."

"Please," she says. "Hiro wouldn't know an anteater from an elephant. Unless it's related to cars or soccer, he's an imbecile."

Chuckling, we lift our burritos to our mouths and take our individual bites. "I think I'm going to bring him tonight," I say.

Her eyes bulge. "Elijah?"

"Yeah."

"Really? Why isn't Cristian coming?"

"He's got a date."

"Oh…" She puckers her lips. "That makes sense."

"Yeah…"

Twisting one of her coiled curls, she seems to think for a moment. "I mean, yeah, bring him." Another pause. "It's not going to be weird for you?"

"Why would it be weird for me? He wants to hang. And we're just getting drinks, right? It's only Hiro and Erica and a few others, right?"

"Yeah, but..." She trails off. "Min's going to be there. You know how fucking nosy she is. What are you going to introduce him as?"

"Oh, I don't know." I say. "*Elijah* maybe?"

Kate sits up. "Sorry. I'm just surprised, that's all. You've never introduced me to any of your other boy toys."

I smile. "First time for everything."

She smiles back and starts collecting our trash. "Well, I'm sad I won't get to see Cristian but I'm looking forward to meeting this Elijah cutie."

My cheeks get warmer. The truth is, I'm looking forward to Kate meeting him too. I'm looking forward to *everyone* meeting him. I have this weird need to show Elijah off. Plus, I'm genuinely curious to see how he interacts with my friends.

The rest of the workday goes by surprisingly fast. It's surprisingly productive, too. I manage to finish a Chinese press release translation that's not due until Tuesday. Elijah texts me just after five o'clock. *There's no dress code, is there?*

No, no. It's just a bar and a few of my friends.

The bar, which is also a French restaurant, is walking distance from our office in Midtown East. When six o'clock rolls around, Kate and I meet Hiro outside our building and head over. Once there, the three of us join Kate's friend, Erica, who has laid claim to a semi-secluded spot in the back. We order our first round of beers.

An hour into our little get-together, I'm examining Hiro's new weed pen when Elijah sends me another text. *Be there in five.* Returning the gadget to Hiro, I head for the exit so I can meet Elijah outside. He doesn't know anyone tonight and I want him to feel comfortable. I also want to be by his side when he makes an entrance.

Elijah shows up in a white T-shirt and tiny running shorts. His muscular arms and thick thighs are out for the world to admire. A duffel bag hangs from his shoulder. When I lay my eyes on him, I feel myself blush at how obscenely sexy he looks. Especially since this is such a departure from his usual, classy style. "Damn, boy," I say, taking in every last inch of his body. "Looking *good.*"

A frown forms on his face. "You said there's no dress code."

"There isn't."

"Should I run home and change?"

"Absolutely not."

"I did shower, FYI."

I think about Elijah all sweaty from the gym. "I kind of wish you didn't."

When we walk in, my hand on the small of Elijah's back, Kate and Hiro are both conveniently hovering near the entrance. "Hi!" she says, bolting over and leaving Hiro in the dust. "I'm Kate." As Elijah shakes her hand, she slides her gaze down his body. "I had no idea this French restaurant served all-American beef, too."

Elijah laughs, as do I, bubbling with delight on the inside, especially when Kate shoots me a nod of approval.

The way Elijah carries himself, his eloquence during small

talk, the attention he's able to command in this setting—one I've never seen him in since we only ever hang out one-on-one—make me desire him even more than usual. The whole night, my hand is possessively placed somewhere on his body. His back. His forearm. His thigh. I sneak in kisses whenever I can. The envy in my friends' eyes only feeds my boldness.

Whenever I'm at a social gathering with Cristian, I also love basking in all the compliments and approving glances. But those are based in respect and adoration. Cristian's my age, we've been together for a long time. Elijah's young, full of contagious energy, the world is his oyster. In many ways, he's my opposing force and having him by my side defies logic. As a result, there's an aroma of scandal in the air. With Cristian, I feel like I'm envied because I'm following the rules. In Elijah's case, it's because I'm breaking them. Breaking the rules is always more fun.

At one point, while Elijah's in the bathroom, Min, a tall Korean girl Kate used to work with at her previous job, shimmies closer to me and says, "Oh my God! Cute guy!"

"Thank you!" I reply.

"So cuuute!" she repeats. Min likes to elongate her words but tonight they're even longer because she's had a few glasses of rosé.

"He's pretty smokin'," Hiro agrees.

"And young!" Min adds.

"He is that too, yes," I mumble.

"How young?"

"Twenty-two."

"Oh my God!" she exclaims. "He's a *baby*!"

"Shh!" Kate scolds.

Min's expression turns pokerfaced. She looks me in the eye.

"What happened with you and Cristian?" she asks. "I thought you were going to have an actual baby and everything. Are you getting a divorce?"

"No, no," I say. "I'm still with him. We're just open."

She blinks. "Open?"

"Yeah. We're in an open marriage."

Her jaw dips. "Ohhh."

"Yup..."

"Wow. I didn't know! That's so crazy!"

"What exactly is so crazy about it?" Kate challenges.

"I mean, how does that even *work*?" Min says.

Kate lets out a tsk. "Google it when you get home?"

Min narrows her eyes at Kate. I do my best to contain my smile. With a contrived snicker, Hiro says, "How does any relationship work, am I right?"

"Anyway," Min says, turning back to me. "I'm super jealous."

You should be, I think as my eyes wander over to where Elijah is now exiting the bathroom. He beams his enchanting smile at a middle-aged woman, who, in turn, melts under it and gives him a shy curtsy before slipping inside the bathroom in his place.

"Be right back." I leave Min with Kate and Hiro and beeline for Elijah.

"Let's get out of here," I whisper into his ear.

"You sure?" he asks.

"Positive."

We say our goodbyes and make our way toward the subway, hands entwined, streetlamps and storefronts illuminating our flushed cheeks and smiles. I'm nuzzling Elijah's neck. "You were amazing," I say into it. "Everyone loved you."

"Really?" he says. "I kind of hated them all."

I squeeze his ass. "Shut up."

He laughs. "They were all lovely. Especially Kate."

At the entrance to the subway, I twist his robust, wrestler-like body to face me and press our crotches together. "Your place?"

Sighing, he shakes his head. "My roommate's got some people over tonight."

I check the time on my phone. It's nearing 10 p.m. According to the text update Cristian has sent me a few minutes ago, he'll be home in an hour.

Elijah says, "Maybe we should just call it a night?"

My eyes flick up. "Really?"

"Yeah. We don't have to have sex every single time we see each other, you know. You're more than just a dick to me, Greg."

At that, I relax my grip around his waist. It's like his words have stamped a seal of approval on a document I wasn't even aware I'd been drafting. "Yeah?" I ask.

"Of course."

"Nothing's going to change?"

He laughs. "Nothing. I promise."

A warm, pleasant sensation spreads through my body. Part of me is afraid to break our routine but another part is thrilled. For some reason, Elijah's words make me happier than any orgasm he could've given me tonight.

Again, I squeeze him against me. Pressing my lips into his, I slip my hands inside the back of his gym shorts. "Fine," I say. "But, next time, you're wearing these shorts again and you're not allowed to shower."

Elijah snorts. "Deal."

"*And* you're letting me film everything."

Both of his hands travel up to cup my cheeks. Looking me in the eyes, a more serious expression on his face, he says, "Anything you want."

CHAPTER 16

A week later, the mid-July rain forces Kate and me to eat lunch indoors. When we get to our favorite salad place it seems like everyone who's ever stepped foot in Bryant Park and their grandmother is in there. People's umbrellas—some still open, some still dripping wet—make the space feel even smaller than usual. Luckily, after we order, Kate shoos a couple of tweens away from a table and scores us a place to sit.

"I think she hates me," Kate says, pushing a forkful of spinach into her mouth.

"Who?"

"Um, Adriana?" She glares at me. "Hiro's cousin? The person I've been talking to you about for the past *fifteen* minutes?"

"Oh," I say, "Sorry. Go on."

"What's with you today?"

I spear some arugula. "Sorry," I repeat. "It's just...I've been trying to hang with Elijah these past few days and he's been blowing me off."

"What? You just saw him a week ago when we all hung out."

"Yeah, but I tried hanging with him this past Saturday and

he had plans. I suggested tonight and he had plans again."

"Maybe it's because, you know, he has *plans*?"

I shake my head. "No, he's definitely acting weird."

"Um. Are you sure you're not overthinking this?" She gives me a knowing look. "You do that, sometimes."

"No. Something's changed."

"Well," Kate says, "maybe this is a good thing."

My eyes snap up. "What do you mean?"

"You have to stop seeing him soon anyway, no?" She shrugs. "The longer you wait, the harder it's going to get."

I shove a bunch of leaves in my mouth and start chewing. Outside, the rain seems to be getting worse. For a moment, we both eat in silence, listening to its spatter and to the cacophony of conversations around us.

"Look," Kate says. "You're obviously infatuated with this boy—as any of us would be! He's young, smart, he's a gentleman, he's a hottie. I get it. *But.*" She pauses. "It's time to let him go, honey. Before things get complicated."

A chilling sense of clarity settles over me as I realize how right she is. Elijah hasn't just been spending a lot of time with me in person. He's been spending a lot of time in my thoughts as well. "I know," I mumble. "I should…"

"Not 'should'. Do it! This is your chance. All I hear lately is 'Elijah, Elijah, Elijah.' When was your last lunch date?"

"It's been a while…"

"*Exactly.* Go fuck someone else for a change. Shit, go to Fire Island, fuck everyone there. It's summer in New York. Live it up. While you still can. You've been spending way too much time with this kid."

"You're probably right…"

"I *am* right."

"Ugh," I say. "Did I get too attached?

"I think you kind of did."

I shake my head. "This has never happened before."

"Well, you've never been faced with impending monogamy and babies before either. You're about to enter a new phase of your life. It's scary, I get it."

I sigh. "Cristian does always say I have a hard time with change..."

"Not just Cristian," she says, flatly. "We all say that."

"Thanks..."

She snickers. "You'll be fine. So you caught a whiff of feelings for one of your boys. Not a big deal. I'm sure it happens a lot in open relationships. But you need to move on." She gives my arm a gentle poke. "And I'm not just saying this because I love Cristian, either," she says. "You need to take a step back, see the big picture again."

As usual, Kate's got a point. I'm behaving like a lovesick teenager. And over who? A temporary fuck buddy? I have a husband, a baby on the way, responsibilities. Like she says, I have to step back, regain the correct perspective. It's too late to organize a sexy lunch date for today but I can probably still set something up for after work.

"Thanks, hon," I say.

"Anytime."

The first thing I do when I get back to the office is let Cristian know I won't be home until late. He quickly responds with: *Okay, have fun.* Once I have his blessing, I fire up Grindr. For an hour after that, when my boss isn't looking, I'm navigating three different conversations with three different guys. I come out on the other side with plans to grab a drink with a twenty-six-year-old engineer named Sam. But since Sam is not available until 8 p.m., I decide to go to the gym before I see him.

After my workout, when I hit the showers, the handsome forty-something-year-old man with long hair with whom I've exchanged a hefty amount of eye contact in the free weights area chooses to, coincidentally, wash up at the same time as I do and in the stall opposite mine.

He leaves his curtain halfway open. Every few seconds, through the small gap in mine, I watch his lathered up, muscular body and curved, semi-erect cock pop in an out of view. Eventually, I think: why the hell not. For all I know, Sam, the guy I have plans with, could turn out to be a total bust. This, here, is an opportunity. I open my own curtain a bit wider and retreat back under the showerhead.

First, I hear the water in his stall turn off. Next, it's the sound of my curtain sliding completely shut. Finally, two solid arms enclose my waist.

We don't speak. We just go through the motions: Me on my knees, water gushing into my eyes. Him on his. Me with my face pressed up against the wall, the prod of his tongue inside me. It's all very mechanical.

When he stands up and tries to push the tip of his cock inside me too, I turn around and shake my head. There's no way I'm letting a rando fuck me without a condom. And with all that water friction? I drop to my knees and stare up into his eyes. He nods in approval and begins to furiously stroke his cock. But I'm not actually swallowing a rando's load either, so, when his face scrunches up, signifying he's close, I lift myself higher. He cums on my chest. A second later I cum on the drain.

Standing, I put on a "phew, that was hot" face, even though, at best, the experience was a four out of ten. By now, all aggression has evaporated from the man's features. He seems flustered and kind of sweet as he gives me a shy smile. For a moment, I wonder what his story might be, whether I should ask for his number.

But I don't. I return to my locker to change, cancel on Sam the engineer boy, and text Elijah instead: *What time are you going to be done with your plans?*

Elijah responds fairly quickly with: *Almost done. Why?*

Want to get a night cap with me?

I bite into my lip as I wait for his answer.

Sure, he says.

Chapter 17

On the plane to California, en route to my cousin's wedding, Cristian lets me have the window seat. He settles himself into the middle one and an elderly South Asian man with a shiny, bald head drops his round body into the third seat by the aisle.

Cristian spins my way and I snicker at the exasperation on his face. We've been hoping that our neighbor would either be the handsome blond bookworm who sat near us by the gate, or the cute Latino with the goatee from the line. Alas, it's neither.

Hope It's a Hot Guy is a game—if you can even call it that—which Cristian and I play every time we travel. There's not much to it. Just the shared giddy anticipation of potentially being seated next to a cutie and, on the rare occasion that it actually happens, the mutual satisfaction and giddy celebration that it did.

The very first time I pointed out a hot guy to Cristian, about a year after Cristian and I officially started dating, he got really pissed off.

"How can you say something like that to your boyfriend?" he said.

"Why shouldn't I?"

"Because you're with *me*. You're not supposed to be lusting after other men."

"Says who?"

"Says the world," he answered. "Says civilization and human history. Or, in the very least, you're not supposed to tell me about it."

"That's not true about the history. And, what? We're allowed to think it, but we're not allowed to talk to each other about it?"

"No," he said.

"It's natural to feel attraction towards attractive people, Cristian. Why should we pretend otherwise? It's nothing to be ashamed of."

"It's not what you do when you're in a relationship with someone."

"That's a groundless rule some puritanical asshole came up with and you know it," I said. "You thinking about other guys, Cristian, doesn't bother me because I know I mean more to you than they ever could. Because I believe in us and in what we have."

That day, Cristian insisted on dropping the subject. But I know it stayed with him. I actually attribute the moment to planting a seed. The seed that made him begin to view sex in a different light. Or, at least, helped him begin to understand the way *I* viewed it.

I steal Cristian's hand and wedge our entwined fingers between our seats. We hold hands while the attendant passes by to make sure we're buckled up.

I lock eyes with him. "Te quiero," I mouth.

"Te quiero," he mouths back.

Two years ago, my cousin, John, moved to San Francisco for work and started dating a Chinese-American woman named Yuen, whom I have yet to meet. They'll be tying the knot in a picturesque seaside hotel in Northern California. The wedding is on Sunday but Cristian and I arrive three days early so we can see and experience The Golden City. Neither of us has ever been before.

The first thing we do when we get to SFO is pick up our rental car. Driving was a huge part of both Cristian's life and mine before we moved to New York, where owning a car is more of a hindrance than a benefit. I drove myself to high school and most of college. Then, in Spain, Cristian's beat-up Mazda took us all over the country and beyond.

"You drive first," Cristian says as we're crossing the parking lot toward our compact-category Nissan. "I want to focus on the scenery."

And what scenery it is. The Bay Area is breathtaking. The vistas put us in a trance but once we get to the city, we quickly snap out of it. It's hard to admire the sights when you're steering the car up hills so steep it's all sky until, all of a sudden, the hood plummets and reveals signs and pedestrians that weren't there before. I nearly have a heart attack every time. "Puta madre," Cristian exclaims with unusual frequency.

Friday night, we go out in the Castro. In New York, Cristian and I don't really frequent gay bars, not if it's just the two of us. Most of our gay and queer friends still live in Spain. From time to time, we might grab a drink at one with Kate and Hiro, but that's about it. When we're travelling, though, the rules are different. Going to gay bars, observing the local queers in their natural habitat is one of our favorite pastimes.

"That whole group is staring at us," I say through my vodka soda, raising my voice so Cristian can hear me over the Lady Gaga song blasting from the speakers.

"I only like the one in the flannel shirt," he says.

"I'd probably do a hit and run on the short one, too."

"What? The short one looks like Liza Minnelli."

I snort. "No, he doesn't." But now that he's said it, I can't unsee it.

"Did you go on Grindr, yet?" Cristian asks.

"No." Between having fun with Cristian and struggling not to check my phone to see if I got a text from Elijah, Grindr didn't even cross my mind. "Did you?"

"No," he says. "Do it now. Let's see what the boys in San Francisco are like."

When Cristian says see, he means see and see only. We don't have threesomes together. They go against Cristian's "not everything in life has to intersect" rule. I'm okay with that. I probably would get a little jealous.

Around midnight, while I'm in the bathroom, Liza Minnelli turns to me at the urinals. "Hi," he says with a sloppy smile.

"Hi," I reply curtly and look back down at my dick. I don't want to act too friendly and give him the wrong idea.

"Is that Latino guy you're with your boyfriend?" he asks.

"Husband."

"Oh..." There's a pause. "He's super sexy. You're lucky."

The brief sting caused by the fact that I'm not the one he's after is quickly replaced with an enormous sense of pride.

"I know," I say. "I am."

Cristian and I may not have threesomes together, but another thing we always do when we travel—without fail, every time—is have sex with each other. In New York, we can go for months without being physically intimate, but give us fresh-smelling hotel sheets and a big bed and we turn into a pair of bonobos in heat.

Tonight, fueled by the closeness of our daytime adventures and the thirst Liza had expressed for Cristian, I am extra attracted to my husband.

When we return to our room, just shy of 2 a.m., Cristian launches himself face first onto the bed. He grunts when I land on top of him. We lie like that for a good minute, by the end of which, I'm rock hard. Cristian can tell. He flips over.

Kissing Cristian, putting my mouth on his body, is like revisiting an old neighborhood. Everything's the same but not quite. It rings completely familiar, yet you see things in a new light, from a new perspective that only time away could grant. Sometimes, you even stumble upon things that have popped up while you were gone and you're given an opportunity to get to know them from scratch.

Since we opened up the marriage, for example, I've noticed a spike in the usage of the English language on Cristian's part. It used to be that the only words that came out of his mouth during any type of physical intimacy with me were Spanish ones. Now, there's a good amount of "oh yeahs" in between his "sis" and I'm kind of into it. It's a welcome new ingredient to our tried-and-true recipe.

I love Cristian's hairy thighs. I love playing peek-a-boo with his foreskin and the way he shudders when I tease his extra-sensitive nipples. But most of all, I love the way he smells to me. Like my twenties. Like Spain. Like comfort and like trust.

Early on Sunday, we check out from our hotel and drive north over the Golden Gate Bridge. The seaside resort where my cousin's having his wedding is over three hours away but it takes us even longer to get there because Northern California is stunning. The giant trees, the idyllic streams, the jutting cliffs, the famously scenic Pacific Coast Highway. It's impossible not to stop along the way to take in the sights and a shit-ton of photos in the process. I'd stop the car even more often if weren't for the fact that my mom keeps calling every twelve minutes asking where we are.

"If she doesn't stop I'm turning around and driving us back to New York."

"She's just excited to see you," Cristian says as he taps a reply in my place because I'm too scared to take my eyes off the road. One mishap and we could go flying over the edge onto the jutting rocks in the ocean below.

"No," I say. "She's excited to see *you*."

I'm not joking. My mother's in love with Cristian. The same woman who, when I was young ingrained in me so much disgust toward gay people that the first time I ever went to a gay bar I was actually repulsed to drink a cocktail prepared for me by the gay bartender, is now in love with my gay husband. My gay *brown* husband at that.

"Your destination is on the left," our navigation system says. I slow the car down. The name of the venue—carved into a beautiful wooden billboard—comes into view. I turn into the gravel road just past it.

Before I even manage to shut the engine off, my mother is already charging down the hill the hotel sits upon, her heels digging into the grass and gravel. Cristian gets out to greet her. Once she's done planting a million kisses on his cheeks, she turns to me and does the same, although with much less abandon.

"I can't believe you're only staying one night," she complains. "Everyone keeps asking about you. You're such a recluse."

"Hi, Mom."

"Did you apologize to your cousin for missing the welcome dinner last night?"

"I did. I also told him I couldn't make it in the RSVP months ago."

"But you *could* have made it. You just didn't."

"It's my fault, Agnes," Cristian jumps in. "I really wanted to see San Francisco."

My mother turns her head toward him and gives him a sad smile. "Oh, my precious Cristian. You don't have to lie. I know my son hates me."

I roll my eyes. Even though I've repeatedly told her otherwise, my mom is still convinced, to this day, that the reason I left the States for Spain so soon after coming out, was due to my parents' unsupportive reaction. That could very well have been the case—our home wasn't the coziest of environments after I told them—and I can see how she'd think that, but I'd wanted to live abroad since way before I came out. But my mom is the star of her own story, so I guess the idea that it was a coincidence which—once again—had nothing to do with her, is too hard for her to swallow.

"Where's Dad?" I ask.

"He's with your brother."

Her arm in Cristian's, she leads us up the hill. I follow with our baggage.

The ceremony starts in less than two hours so Cristian and

I check in and head over to our room to change into our suits. Along the way, we bump into uncle George on the stairs and my cousin Nora and her twin second-graders—Jon and Cam—in the hallway. The entire building seems to be overrun by my clan.

As I watch Cristian exchange handshakes, hugs, and smiles, a strange thought enters my mind. I imagine Elijah in Cristian's place. I envision my relatives meeting him for the first time. "He's so polite, Greg," Aunt Denise would say. "How'd you score that young piece of ass?" Uncle George would tease. I indulge in the fantasy for only a moment longer before it makes me feel too guilty and I fling it away.

In our room, we hear an unrelenting knock on our door. Cristian opens it and my dad and brother spill inside. "You're not butt-fucking in here are, you?" my brother asks, rushing over to sweep Cristian into a big bear hug. "Ew, what are you wearing?" he says when he gets to me. "Mr. Big Shot New York-er is too cool for a normal tux?"

"Oh, look," I say, embracing him. "Your bald spot's bigger."

"Where's your baby mama?" he says, pretending to search the room for Amelia.

"Why would she be here?"

"Aren't you guys, like, one of those throuples now?"

"Yes," I reply, flatly. "Because that's how surrogates work."

My brother slaps my arm. "I can't believe you're going to be a dad! And so soon! Never really pictured you as one, to be honest. Cristian? Yes. You? No."

"Thanks."

My father pulls out a bottle—yes a whole bottle—of whiskey from within the jacket of his suit. The bottle is not full. "We need to have a welcome drink," he says.

"No, we don't," I say. "How about we drink *after* the ceremony."

"Ridiculous! We're at a wedding! Come! Before the womenfolk get here."

I stick to my decision and pass with a stubborn shake of my head. My brother does the same. But Cristian, being Cristian and not wanting to leave my dad hanging, steps up to the plate with a big smile. He accepts the bottle and takes a big swig. "Yeah! Amigo!" my brother, who does not speak Spanish, cheers.

Pleased, my dad pats Cristian on the back. My heart swells with both love and gratitude. Cristian fits in with my family so well. He knows them, understands them. He's seen me fight with my brother. Helped carry my dad to bed after he passed out drunk. Witnessed my mom's multiple breakdowns. He belongs here with us. With me.

The wedding ceremony takes place on top of a cliff overlooking the ocean. It's a bit windy, but it's a beautiful scene nonetheless. My cousin's bride, Yuen, looks both glamorous and graceful in her flowing, white dress.

The vows are pretty basic but get the job done. As they're happening, I reach over and hold Cristian's hand. Cristian and I never really had what you'd call a wedding. Four days after we moved to the States from Spain, we went to the city hall with only my mom as a witness and had some family and friends over for a BBQ afterwards.

In the ballroom, after the ceremony, I finally get to meet and congratulate the bride. "Ah, so you're the handsome gay cousin living it up in New York with the handsome Spanish artist husband," she says, giving me a big hug.

"That's me."

"And you speak Mandarin I heard?"

"Yes, ma'am."

"We'll see about that," she says with a wink as a tiny older woman attempts to whisk her away, "Oh!" she adds. "Congratulations on the pregnancy!"

"Thank you!"

A little later, Cristian invites Mom to dance. I'm left behind with my brother, his wife Gina, and Dad—who's surprisingly lucid considering how much he's had to drink. Bowls of noodles and tofu, plates of dumplings and stir-fried bok choy—so many intricate dishes adorn the table surface you can barely see the white tablecloth underneath.

"Everything okay over there in the Big Apple?" Dad yells into my ear over a Chinese pop number. Out on the dance floor, Cristian is throwing my mother this way and that. A small crowd of spectators has gathered around them to cheer.

"Of course," I shout back, my eyes on my husband, a big smile on my lips. "Everything's perfect."

CHAPTER 18

The movie Elijah and I were supposed to see starts in fifteen minutes. It's a new feel-good romantic comedy with some supposed timely social commentary. I had been looking forward to it. I thought he was, too. But then, less than two hours ago, Elijah informed me that he "couldn't make it after all." The reason? "Work."

Okay. Understandable. Work is important. I can get behind that. Except ten minutes ago, I saw that he was active on Grindr. He must be *very* busy.

The theater where the movie is playing is in Times Square. I have no intention of seeing it alone, but since Times Square is a walkable distance from Midtown East, where I work, and since my plans have gone down the drain, I go anyway.

Normally, a seasoned New Yorker would tell you to avoid Times Square like the plague. Times Square, they'd say, is only for tourists and the shady, overpriced facilities that cater to them. Well, I'd say that, yes, this is all true, but that's exactly why it's worth a visit. Because—and I have plenty of experience to support this—Times Square is also a fertile land of fresh, international cuties. And since Times Square is also a hotbed of hotels in all sorts of price ranges, cuties who *can host* on top of that.

Wandering through the infamous district of humongous billboard screens, Elmo costumes, and human garbage, I fire up Grindr and scroll through the menu of faces and torsos. Okay, this guy's hot. As is this one. See? Who needs Elijah?

Within a minute, I receive a message from a well-proportioned, twenty-four-year-old sporting an Irish flag in his profile. Right away, I decide that he'll more than do. In the very least, I won't have to worry about a language barrier.

Hey, cutie, I write. *Hosting?*

No, sorry, he writes back. *Staying with mates. You?*

My enthusiasm tumbles. *Maybe*, I say, ready to move on to the next guy, but then I notice that he's only two hundred feet away. *Where are you?*

Don't laugh, he replies. *I'm at an Irish pub.*

I look up from my screen and, down the street, see the big neon clover. *Seriously?* I ask.

Not my idea, I swear. A sweating emoji.

I send a laughing emoji back. *Are you able to get away?*

Yeah. Just tell me where to go and I'm there.

Just come outside.

A couple of minutes later, when he does, he appears looking slightly flustered—or maybe just tipsy—with red cheeks. His hands are deep in his pockets but there's a certain swagger to his walk and the grin on his face is one of confidence. He's definitely an attractive one, this one. My stomach flips with delight.

"Greg," I say, sticking out my hand.

"Connor," he replies.

Half an hour later, Connor and I are at yet another Irish

pub (Times Square is swarming with them, for some reason) sitting across from each other on high stools. Our knees keep bumping under the table. By now, I know that Connor works as an assistant for some startup CEO in Dublin, that he's in town for three more days, and that he's hoping to permanently move to New York sometime soon.

"…in Kips Bay, probably."

"What?"

Connor's smile falters. "Kips Bay. That's where I'd like to live. After I move."

"Right. Sorry."

"Everything all right?" Connor asks.

"Yup!" I clear my throat. "Your friends are all out at that pub right now, yeah?"

Connor looks down at his beer. "Yeah, but I really can't have guests in our room…Sorry. They might come back at any time." A pause. His fingers start stroking the side of his half-empty mug. "How far is, uh, your place?"

"Far," I say because Cristian's home tonight. There's no way I can invite this kid over. "But I have an idea," I say, just as one hits me. Connor's eyes light up. "*Someone* is bound to have a room around here that we could borrow, no?" I raise my phone in the air. "Do you mind if I do some quick research?"

Connor's shoulders stiffen. I'm taking a risk here and I know it. Finally, slowly, he nods in understanding.

While I'm furiously replying to all the Grindr messages I've received in the past half hour, I ask, "You don't mind if I send out your pics too, do you?"

Connor shrugs. "No, go ahead." And with his permission, I get right to it. "I've never done that before, by the way," I hear him add.

I look up from my screen. He's watching me, his cheeks the most potent shade of red yet. "A threesome, you mean?" I ask.

Connor looks around nervously. "Yeah."

I drop my gaze back to my phone. "Well," I say, "you might not have to."

"What do you mean?"

I angle the screen his way. "This guy is staying just across the street," I explain. Connor glances at the photo I'm showing him and his face scrunches up. It's the reaction I expect. "Yeah," I go on. "Not my type, either. But I sent him your photo and asked if he wants to watch us. Just watch. Nothing more. He said yes."

Connor's eyes turn into saucers. "You did all this just now?"

"Yup. We can basically use his room as we please."

Connor's hand travels to the back of his neck. "This is crazy."

"Why?" I ask. "Who cares if he watches?" I'm trying to sound nonchalant, but inside I'm begging for him to agree.

"I don't know…"

I knock my knee into his. "Come on," I say. "Live a little." *Please*, I think. *I need this.* "If you're at all uncomfortable, we'll leave."

He bites his bottom lip. But then smiles. "All right, fuck it."

The hotel where our generous host is staying—which really is just diagonally across the street from the Irish pub—is easy to miss. The building, connected on both sides to other buildings, is super narrow. It looks like it's barely surviving the fight to maintain its slice of Times Square real estate. It also looks like its lobby will require us to get past the check-in counter in order to reach the elevators.

"What do we say if they stop us?" Connor asks nervously.

"They won't."

"But what if they do?"

"Then we'll tell them the truth: that we're here to see our buddy in room 604." I consider adding that I've visited lots of hotels in my time and that I've never been stopped once. In fact, I think I've even been to *this* very hotel before. A Russian finance guy, I believe, two or three years ago. But I don't say this because I don't want Connor to know that this is what I do on a regular basis.

He takes a deep breath. "Okay."

At some hotels, you need a room card to work the elevators. In those cases, you have to wait for an actual guest or a bellboy to ride with you. Thankfully, this hotel isn't one of them. I urge Connor to get in the elevator first and slip in behind him.

As soon as the elevator doors shut, I push him up against the wall. But our first kiss is not as electric as I was hoping it would be. In fact, outside of the meaty presence of someone's tongue wrestling with mine, I don't feel anything at all. Connor's lips and tongue are just that, lips and a tongue. If I'm being honest, I'd rather be kissing Elijah. Wait, *Cristian*. I mean Cristian. Elijah can go fuck himself.

Our "buddy" in room 604—a quiet-looking, Middle Eastern man in his early forties wearing a bathrobe—opens the door with some reluctance, but once his eyes take us both in, he noticeably relaxes. "You're real," he says.

"As are you," I reply, trying my best not to stare at the numerous hairs jutting out of his nose. I extend my hand. "I'm Greg," I say. "And this is my buddy, Connor." Behind me, Connor gives the man a small wave.

The man clears his throat. "Yosef," he replies with a reserved smile and steps aside. Connor follows me in and finds a spot by the wall, just inside the door, as if to ensure an easy escape route.

"Thanks for having us over," I say.

"Of course," Yosef replies. "Who wouldn't?" His room has a typical business hotel vibe. A plastic suitcase with a JFK destination tag sits open in the middle of the carpet. There's an open beer on the nightstand.

"Are you in New York for work?" I ask. "Pleasure?"

Yosef's still standing where he closed the door. My guess is he's Israeli. Or maybe Lebanese. "The former," he says.

"What do you do?"

"I work for an airline."

"Cool. Are you a flight attendant?"

He shakes his head.

"Pilot?"

He shakes his head again. Since he doesn't elaborate, I don't press. He's too meek to be a pilot, anyway. He's probably some kind of engineer.

I indicate the bed. "Do you mind?" I ask.

"No," Yosef replies, eyes bulging with excitement. "Go ahead."

I sit on the edge and nod to Connor. He shuffles over and sits beside me. Our host settles himself on the other end, by the headboard. The bed is king-sized so it's big enough to provide a respectful amount of distance between us.

Connor and I kiss. Yosef leans back, making himself more

comfortable. He opens up his robe, its flaps falling to both sides, and sticks his hand down his boxer briefs.

"You okay?" I ask Connor when I see that he's quite tense.

"Yeah," he answers. His breaths are quick and short.

I look over at Yosef. The hand in his underwear is now moving around. "No touching, okay?" I remind him. He shoots off a few rapid nods of agreement.

After a minute, Connor loosens up. His tongue gets hungrier, his lips more audacious. I pull his shirt over his head and push him back on the bed. By now, Yosef's unusually girthy cock is poking out of the slit in his boxers. He's stroking it in an unusual way too, starting at the base and sliding his hand up toward the tip in measured movements that remind me of squeezing out toothpaste.

Straddling Connor's thighs, I press his wrists down with my hands and run my lips down his neck, his pale chest, then farther still. I stick my left hand in my pants, forcing my own cock to wake the fuck up.

It doesn't.

Again, I stand, this time pulling Connor up with me until his face is level with my crotch. Over at the other end of the bed, Yosef appears hypnotized by our performance. My breathing intensifies. A film of sweat now covers my body. I form a fist around Connor's soft hair. But right away, all I can think about is how it's so much longer and different in texture compared to Elijah's. The thought is extremely distracting. I grit my teeth as hard as I can, hoping to squeeze Elijah out of my brain.

A few forceful thrusts of my hips later, Connor's mouth still isn't helping.

This isn't going to happen.

Panting, I take a step back. "I think I'm going to go."

By the headboard, Yosef freezes.

"What's wrong?" Connor asks, looking up at me.

I'm pulling up my pants. "I have to go," I say. "I'm sorry."

Connor gives me a dejected nod and starts gathering his clothes.

"Leaving?" Yosef asks, wrapping himself back up in the flaps of his robe.

"Yeah," I say. "Sorry. I don't think I like being watched after all." It's a complete lie, of course. Being watched has nothing to do with it.

"Wait," Connor calls. "I'm coming, too." I stop, just before opening the door. The least I can do is wait for Connor so we can leave together.

"Sorry," I say again to Yosef.

Yosef gives me a patient nod. "It's all right," he replies. "Take care."

The elevator ride down is a stark contrast to the ride up from earlier. Again, Connor and I are the only people in it, but, this time, he's at one wall and I'm at another. To his credit, he doesn't sprinkle me with questions.

"I'm sorry for fucking up your night," I say when we get outside.

"No worries."

"This has nothing to do with you. You're a wonderful guy."

"Don't worry about it, really." He pauses for a second before adding; "I'm in town for a few more days. Maybe we can grab a drink tomorrow?"

"Yeah," I say, but there's little conviction in my voice.

I think Connor can tell. "I'll send you my WhatsApp," he

says, but there's very little conviction in his voice now, too. "Hit me up whenever."

I return his small smile. "Will do."

As I walk to the train, I tell myself that Connor will be just fine. He's going to chat up a new American guy on Grindr and he's going to forget all about me. I'll be fine too. Five minutes in my husband's presence and I'll be in a much better mood.

I think it's time for a break. I've been having way too much random sex and way too many thoughts about Elijah. Maybe it's even time to call it early quits on both. These are the actions and mindset of an insecure guy in his twenties seeking validation. Or a depressed dude with only a few months left to live. Not a happy father-to-be with a wonderful life partner waiting for him at home.

I picture it all in my head. Me, walking through the door. Cristian by his easel, or maybe on the couch with his laptop. Me, smiling a huge smile of relief. Cristian, seeing it and smiling back. "You're home early," he'll say.

But when I finally do reach our place, slip my key in our lock and open the door, Cristian's not on the couch. Someone else is.

My skin goes cold. What I see in my home in that very moment is so surreal, so unexpected, so farfetched that, at first, I don't even process it as something real. For a few beats, I'm stuck in a dream. A bad, uncomfortable, disconcerting dream. It's only when Cristian steps out of the bathroom, buffing his wet hair with a towel, his limp dick dangling, that I have no choice but to accept that I'm very much awake.

"Oh," Cristian says, his face opening wide with surprise. "You're home early." From me, he turns to look at the man on my couch, in my living room, in my home.

But the man is looking at me, not at Cristian. There's an eerie smirk on his lips. Those same lips I've kissed multiple times before.

"Hi, Greg," Russell says. "Good to see you again."

CHAPTER 19

"What the fuck?"

"Sorry," Cristian says to me, wrapping the towel he's holding around his naked waist. "I thought you'd be out much later."

"What are you doing in my house?" I demand, my gaze locked on Russell and his neat beard and his blue eyes and, most importantly, on his smug grin, which—as soon as Cristian turns his head in Russell's direction—quickly disappears.

"I was just about to leave," Russell replies.

"Why are you *here*?" I repeat with more force. Russell's oddly calm and not at all surprised to see me. I feel like I'm the only one here who doesn't know what's going on. Even Cristian is acting like these are the most natural circumstances in the world.

Russell opens his mouth to speak but Cristian interrupts him. "I was going to tell you," he says to me, taking a step closer.

On instinct, I take a step back. "Tell me what?"

Cristian half-shrugs, the golden brown skin of his naked torso still glistening in spots from his shower. "The two of you know each other, right?"

At that, Russell stands up from the couch. "We sure do," he says. His hand lifts into a wave. A very condescending one. Or, at least, that's how it feels to me.

"Dude," I say to him, suddenly extremely tired. I just wanted to come home to my husband. I didn't sign up for this. Whatever this even is. "What are you doing?"

"Can we just sit down and talk about this like adults?" Cristian offers, trying to sound upbeat. "Let me open up a bottle of wine." He starts toward the kitchen.

"There's nothing to talk about," I say. "I fucked this guy." But then Cristian's words catch up to me. "Wait, he *told* you about that?"

"Yes," Cristian answers. "Of course."

My stomach drops. "And you're okay with it?"

Cristian's Adam's apple goes up and down. "Well, we figured it out later on…"

"*Later on?*" I squeak. "How many times have you seen each other?"

Russell's voice is firm. "Quite a few times," he says. A cold shudder passes through my body. Something about his quiet, restrained demeanor feels really off.

"One night, while we were talking," Cristian explains, gesticulating with his arms a little more than usual—he tends to do that when he's nervous, "I mentioned you and Russell connected the dots."

"The translator thing tipped me off," Russell adds with a smile, like he's just conveying a fun tidbit of information.

"You're a fucking liar," I say, but Russell doesn't even flinch. It's like he expects me to react like this. I turn to Cristian. "Look," I say to him, "mi amor, this guy is just an entitled creep with a grudge. He got mad because I broke things off with him. He obviously just wants to get back at me by fucking you."

"Greg," Russell says, "I swear to you, I had no idea that Cristian—"

"Mi amor," I go on, raising my voice to drown out Russell's, "he did a search on you while I was seeing him. Or maybe even before. He knew your name and your visa status. He knew *exactly* what he was doing when he hit you up."

Cristian holds my gaze. I glance at Russell. He's watching us—watching me—with pure satisfaction. "Actually," Cristian says. "I'm the one who hit *him* up."

A lump forms in my throat. "What?"

"I was on Grindr, I saw him, and I said hi." Cristian shrugs.

"I really didn't know he was your husband until later," Russell adds. "It's not like any of us use our real names on the apps. If I knew, I wouldn't have even replied, considering how you and I ended things."

The room falls silent as hesitation floods my system. Maybe this is, in fact, a coincidence. A fucked up coincidence, for sure, but a coincidence, nonetheless. New York's a big city, but it's not *that* big. It's technically possible that these two met by pure chance, completely outside of my sphere of influence.

"No," I say to Cristian, refusing to accept it. Russell had catfished me. Stalked me even before he'd ever met me. There's no way this is a coincidence. "You might've hit him up first, but I bet you he somehow made sure you would. I wouldn't be surprised if he was hanging around your studio, waiting for you to do it."

One of Cristian's bushy eyebrows rises. He looks to Russell, who shrugs like "yeah, I have no idea what he's talking about either". This is when it hits me. Ever since I walked in through the door, Russell's been nothing but a gentleman.

"Why are you acting like someone you're not?" I accuse him.

Russell's brow knots. "I'm always like this."

"No, you're not."

"I am. I told you. When I called you, remember? With you, I was just a little nervous. Sometimes I get a little carried away when I'm trying to impress my dates."

"You're so full of shit," I hiss. "Just tell Cristian the truth."

Cristian looks back and forth between us. While Cristian's facing me, Russell's smirk makes a comeback.

"Okay," I say, relieved to see that, earlier, I wasn't imagining it. "Get out."

"Greg," Cristian says. "Come on."

Since I never even got a chance to take them off, I march over to Russell in my shoes. I clasp him by his arm and start pulling. "Get the fuck out of my house."

"Greg!" Cristian says, rushing over to separate us. "Joder! Stop it!"

"No. He's lying. He's smirking over at me from behind your back."

"He's not!" Cristian says. "Stop it! You're acting like a maniac."

I whip my face towards Cristian, my jaw clenched. I remind myself that Cristian is the victim in all of this. He doesn't know the real Russell. He's the one being deceived. Still. He's being awfully protective of the creep. There's no reason he shouldn't believe me. I'm his husband. But I don't want us to fight. Not in front of Russell. So, through clenched teeth, I just say, "We agreed not to have guys over at our apartment."

Cristian stands taller. "Hasn't stopped you before."

While I glare at him, trying to convey how serious I am, Russell says, "Look. I'm leaving, okay? I don't want you guys to fight."

All the self-restraint I've managed to accumulate pops. "Pff," I say, "Yeah fucking right. I think that's *exactly* what you want."

"It's really not, Greg. Why do you keep saying that?"

"You know what?" I say, grabbing him again. "I don't even care. Whatever this is, it's done. You can get out of my house now." Again, I start to escort him out. This time, Cristian doesn't get involved. I open the front door. At the threshold, Russell stiffens under my grip and glances over my shoulder at Cristian.

"Bye," he says to him.

"I'm so sorry," Cristian replies.

Russell shrugs and steps into the stairwell. I don't close the door completely. I wait for him to start descending the steps to make sure he's actually leaving. Once he does, he looks back up at me and gives me that stupid grin again. I slam the door shut.

When I turn around, behind the kitchen counter, Cristian's arms are crossed. He's shaking his head and glowering at me with full-on disappointment.

"What?" I challenge.

"That was so unnecessary."

"It was *very* necessary," I say, marching over to our bar cart to grab a bottle of vodka. My hand shakes around it. "The guy's a vengeful creep." I twist off the cap. "He couldn't get what he wanted and now he's trying to get back at me. He was pretending to be this gentleman with you just so something like this, like tonight, would happen. So he could be here when I got back. He planned it all, trust me."

"Why do you think this is all about *you*?"

With a smack, I set a shot glass on our countertop. "Because it clearly is. I'm telling you. He's only doing this out of spite. You don't believe me?"

"I didn't say that."

"Then why are you defending him?"

"Because I like him."

The words are like a silent punch to my gut. Blood rushes to my ears. "Cristian, you can't see him again," I begin, but Cristian just shakes his head and starts toward the bedroom. I stomp after him. "I don't trust that guy one bit."

Cristian's completely naked again, his towel a crumpled pile on our bed. He yanks his pajama pants from under his pillow and starts stepping into them. "I understand this is an unusual situation," he says, "and I understand why it makes you uncomfortable and upset. But we have an agreement until September when Amelia's due. And, until then, *I'll* be the one making decisions about who I see and who I don't see."

"He's just using you!"

"I don't think he is." Cristian's tripping over his words now; his English always gets worse when he's worked up. "He's a sweet guy and I enjoy spending time with him. And I told you. I'm the one who reached out to him. Not the other way around."

"A sweet guy?" This actually takes me aback. "Are you serious? When I hung out with him I couldn't even get a word in. He'd just brag about himself and whom he knows and how rich he is. He wouldn't shut the fuck up."

"He explained that. He said he was just trying too hard to impress you. And, anyway, he's not like that with me."

"Because he's *pretending*," I say. "You want to know exactly

142

what happened with me and him?"

"He already told me."

"You don't want to hear my side of the story?"

Cristian goes quiet. He sucks in a deep breath and sits on the bed, facing me. Still shirtless, he looks at me and waits.

I lean against the doorway, letting my hands fall to my sides. "I went out with him a few times," I start. "I even mentioned him to you at one point—I told you I had a date with a famous TV producer? You don't remember?"

"No."

I narrow my eyes. "Well anyway, I thought he was hot and I wanted to fuck him." Here, I hesitate, but see no reason why I shouldn't tell Cristian the whole truth. I clear my throat. "Especially after I found out that he's never bottomed before…"

Cristian rolls his eyes.

"And he hangs out with all these hot actors so I thought—"

"Jesus, Greg."

"*Anyway*, we had sex. Twice. And that's it. Then I ended it and now he's trying to get back at me for dumping him."

"He said you didn't tell him you were married."

Heat fills my cheeks. "He knew anyway. The whole time. It was creepy."

Cristian's staring me down. "Why didn't you tell him about me?"

I fidget against the doorframe. "Because I knew I wouldn't see him again."

"After you fucked him."

I swallow. "Correct."

"So you weren't honest *and* you basically used him."

"He's an adult. He made the decision to have sex with me

even though he secretly *did* know I was married because he's a stalker. It's not my fault he assumed we were separated or had a green card marriage or something. And who even assumes that?"

Cristian's jaw tightens. "I would."

"No you wouldn't."

"Yes, I would. If I really liked you, I would want to see you in a positive light. I wouldn't think the worst of you."

"Okay," I say. "Fine. I should've been more honest with him. I'll admit it. But that doesn't change the fact that the guy's not right in the head. You know what else he did? He catfished me on Grindr once. Before we ever even met."

Surprise widens Cristian's eyes. "What?"

"Yeah. He pretended to be someone else and led me to a dark, deserted street so he could intimidate me or whatever the fuck he was trying to do."

"He told you this?"

I pause. "I'm sure it was him."

Cristian sighs. "Greg, I'm tired," he says and starts looking for the shirt he sleeps in. "I'm going to bed. Let's talk about this some other time."

"I want to talk about it now."

"No," he says, pulling the T-shirt over his head. "Tonight you're too agitated. Russell was nothing but polite and civil and you literally threw him out of the house."

"Are you going to see him again?"

He stops and glares at me. "If you're so sure that he only wanted to sleep with me to get back at you, then he got what he wanted, no?" He slips under the covers. "By that logic, *he* won't want to see *me*, right?"

He's got a point. "But—"

"Can you hit the light, please?"

Chapter 20

The next morning, I wake up to a text from Elijah. *Sorry about the movie yesterday*, it says. *Are you free tonight? I'd really like to see you.*

Exhaling a long, slow breath, I close my eyes and slap the phone down on the pillow in front of my nose. A minute later, I haul myself up into a sitting position and rub the heels of my hands into my eyes. Beside me, Cristian stirs awake.

"Did the alarm go off?" he asks in a crusty, half-asleep voice. Leaning down, I nibble at his cheek. "Not yet," I whisper. "Go back to sleep."

Last night, after Cristian and I had our fight, I let my husband be. I don't blame him for getting upset. For the remaining two months, he's an adult in an open relationship and he's entitled to see whomever he wants. I came home. I threw a fit. I can see how, to Cristian, I might've come off as a tad jealous and unreasonable. Especially considering how composed and gentlemanly Russell was the entire time.

But that's fine. Cristian can think whatever he wants. As long as he doesn't see that creepy fucker again. And, today, I'm going to make *sure* he doesn't.

At lunch, after she hears the story, Kate says, "Okay, I literally just got the chills. Look." She's not lying. Her brown skin is covered in tiny bumps. She takes a long, contemplative sip of her green smoothie and squints. "I guess it *is* possible that they just like each other...."

"Sure. But it's not *likely*. I don't want this guy anywhere near Cristian."

"I kind of don't either," she agrees. "What are you going to do?"

"I'm going to see him. One on one."

Kate's lips part. "Are you going to tell him to back off?"

"Well, first, I'm going to apologize again for how things ended between us, and then I'm going to *ask* him to back off, like an adult. Man to man. Hopefully, without Cristian there, he'll cut the bullshit."

She nods. "Okay, just be careful. What if he's, like, a psycho who's trying to sabotage your life? Call me if you need backup."

After lunch, I return to my desk and scroll through the contacts in my phone until I find Russell's name. *Let me buy you a drink this week*, I text and wait. I don't suggest a specific time and place because I'm worried that, if I'm too pushy, he might tell me to fuck off or just ignore me altogether. He doesn't reply for an hour. Then for two. After three, I follow up with: *Please*.

A reply pops up almost immediately.

Tonight, it says. *Last place we went to together. 8 p.m.*

A mix of relief and irritation washes over me. I do want to talk to Russell as soon as possible, but, fuck, tonight, I already promised to see Elijah. There's no way I can risk asking Russell to reschedule. He might refuse to give me the time of day again.

146

I could—maybe even should—cancel on Elijah since he cancelled on me yesterday, but I can't bring myself to do it. I guess I'll have to make both appointments work.

I text Elijah to tell him to meet me at a Greek restaurant in Williamsburg. The plan is to eat somewhere near his place so I can walk him home afterwards and invite myself over for a quickie before I venture off to see Russell.

After work, on the way, I realize how nervous I am to see Elijah. And I'm not exactly sure why. But I scold myself for feeling nervous in the first place. Elijah shouldn't be taking up this much of my mental space. He shouldn't be this much of a priority in my life.

But, in the end, when I actually see him, all my nerves and annoyance instantly melt away under the blowtorch of his radiant smile.

He plants a long, hungry kiss on my lips. "Hello, mister."

"Hey, cute stuff."

"I'm sorry about the movie last night," he says. "I shouldn't have cancelled on you like that at the last minute. That was not cool."

"No apologies needed." I swallow. "Everything's all right, though, right?"

"Absolutely."

The whole way to the restaurant and most of the time there, under the table, our hands stay connected. As usual, Elijah catches me up on what's new and listens intently to every little thing I have to say. As usual, there's a moment when he gets so lost in his thoughts, he briefly disappears into another world. And, as usual, his lips stretch into a huge smile when he returns back to ours and finds me beside him.

Sadly, my time with Elijah is not as enjoyable as it could be. Russell's smug grin lingers in the back of my mind like a red-light exit sign at a dark club, constantly reminding me of my much-less appealing appointment number two.

"Can I come up?" I ask, once we're in front of Elijah's apartment building. The steel zigzag ladders of the fire escape loom over our heads.

He waits for a rowdy group of Australians to pass us by before answering. "My roommates are home."

"So? I'll be in and out." I shoot him a wink.

Fighting a smile, he says, "Fine. But we have to be quiet."

We are not quiet. We are the furthest thing from quiet imaginable. Even without our symphony of moans and grunts, Elijah's roommates would know exactly what we're up to just based on the rhythmic thwacking of Elijah's bed against the wall.

For what he put me through yesterday, I fuck him extra hard. It's my way of administering punishment. I also make an extra effort to memorize everything about the moment—his slightly knotted eyebrows, his parted lips, the plea in his eyes. Who knows how many more opportunities to see him like this I have left.

"Are you close?" he breathes. "I'm close."

"I can be." I thrust faster. Droplets of sweat from my forehead fall and hit Elijah's flushed cheeks. "Hold on."

"Tell me when."

"Okay. Now."

Only when we're done and Elijah is wiping himself with a T-shirt from his dirty laundry basket does he feel embarrassed about the noise we made.

"Your roomies are both adults," I assure him. "They don't

care, I promise."

He's sitting on his bed, naked, watching me put my clothes back on. "It's just… I don't know. It's not a very *refined* thing to do."

"Expressing your feelings for another person in a physical way is not a very refined thing to do? That doesn't sound like you." I lean down and kiss him.

Elijah's broad shoulders rise and fall as he sighs. "Where are you running off to so quickly, anyway?" he asks. "Husband duties calling?"

Even though he's just teasing, I feel a nauseating pang. I'm starting to like it less and less when Elijah brings up Cristian. "I have to see an old friend." I say. "Someone I *really* don't want to see, so wish me luck."

Outside, I'm gripped by a powerful sense of annoyance. I could still be cuddling with Elijah right now or heading home to watch a movie with Cristian. But no. I have to go deal with a spiteful asshole.

As the train crosses the Williamsburg Bridge over to Manhattan, I try to remember everything I can about Russell Mailey from our time together. The pompous vibes he gave off, the self-involved stories he told. Jesus. What does Cristian even see in the guy? Beyond the fact that he's conventionally attractive and wealthy and, okay, semi-famous—attributes Cristian's never really cared about—what else is there? From what I know about him, the guy would have to put on quite an act for Cristian to be even remotely attracted to him.

When I get to the bar, Russell's already there, because of course he is, and, of course, I'm four minutes late. A one-sided smirk on his lips, he makes a show of looking at his wristwatch.

"Some things never change, I guess," he says.

I ignore the snide remark and plop onto the stool beside him, where I angle my body his way and cross my arms. "All right," I say. "What's going on?"

Russell makes a face like he's insulted. "Didn't you say you'd buy me a drink?"

Biting my tongue, I raise a hand for the bartender. From the way the man—a handsome, older European with shoulder-length hair—eyes us, I can't help but wonder if he remembers the scene Russell and I had created the last time we were here, when our little break-up and Russell's crying caused quite a stir. Through a humble smile, I order our drinks: a Negroni for me and a whiskey on the rocks for Russell.

"Aw, you remember," he says.

To keep my irritation at bay, I squeeze my eyes shut and try to breathe. I'm going to get straight to the point. There's no need in prolonging this.

"Look, Russell," I say. "I'm sorry I wasn't honest with you about being married and I'm sorry I led you on just so I could sleep with you."

Russell nods. "As you should be."

"I am."

"Good."

"So will you please leave Cristian alone?"

"No."

I squint at him. "What?"

"I said: no."

"What do you mean 'no'?"

"No, I'm not going to leave Cristian alone." Looking me in

the eyes and smirking his smug smirk, he takes a sip of his whiskey. "Better?"

The venom in his voice takes me aback. "Why are you doing this?" I ask.

"Why are you so surprised? Isn't that *your* policy, too? Take what you want when you want it, no questions asked?"

"Look," I say, trying to stay calm. "I apologized. Now, I'm asking you to let me and my husband be. What else do you want me to do?"

"You do whatever you need to do, Greg," he says. I hate how calm he is. "You're making your choices and I'm making mine."

"Stop it," I bark, my anger leaking through the barely-there dam of patience. "Does fucking with my life give you some kind of kick or something? Is that why you catfished me, too? You get off on tormenting me?"

"Catfished you?" he asks, feigning surprise.

"You pretended to be someone on Grindr and you tricked me. Stop acting like you don't know what I'm talking about. I know it was you."

He grins. "Hmm, not quite sure what you're going on about. But maybe if you didn't use Grindr so much, things like that wouldn't happen to you?"

I have an urge to close my fist and pound it into his face. "Dude," I say, much more loudly than I intend to. "Is what I did to you *that* bad?" I can feel the bartender's glare of disapproval. "Just how fucking delicate are you?"

Russell stares at me with those icy blue eyes of his, clearly enjoying my little display of frustration. "Maybe if you actually got to know me, you'd know."

"I *did* get to know you! You're a cocky little self-absorbed douche one minute and a crybaby the next. And, now, you're a grudge-holding *psychopath*."

"Cristian's really handsome," Russell says out of nowhere. He appears completely unbothered by my name-calling. "And he's got such a pure heart. He's a great guy. I can see why you like him so much."

Pinching my lips, I give him a look of pity. "You poor, poor thing," I say. "Even if Cristian decides to see you again—which, after I talk to him today, I guarantee he won't—he'll have to cut you loose in September."

"Ah, yes, the baby," Russell says. "Are you sure you're ready to be a father? If you ask me, you still have a lot of growing and reflecting to do."

My insides start boiling. I could hit him. It's what he wants, I can tell. He'd love to see me turn to violence. But I won't. I won't give him the satisfaction. I told myself I'd be mature tonight and that's exactly how I'm going to behave.

Clenching my jaw, I stare at him in silence and wait for my breathing to stabilize. Then I shoot up to my feet, yank out a twenty from my wallet, and throw it on the bar counter. "Just leave us alone," I say.

And then, just before I turn away, I add: "*Please*."

Chapter 21

"You went to *see* him?" Cristian asks, his features scrunched together. The frying pan he's gripping with his fist unleashes a hiss and a cloud of smoke. "Joder, why can't you just let this go? You're being such a child."

With a clink, my keys drop into the tray by the door. "Mi amor, I went to him to apologize. But, listen, he's only seeing you to piss me off, I'm sure of it now."

Cristian goes back to stir-frying his vegetables. "Great."

"Please don't see him again. He's bitter and unhinged."

For a couple of beats Cristian is silent. Then, he turns off the stove and says, "You know, technically, I know him better than you do."

"What?"

He turns to me and crosses his arms. "I've spent more time with him than you have. You've only seen him…what? A handful of times?"

Scowling, I say, "And? Congratulations? That doesn't change the fact that he's bitter and unhinged."

"I'm just saying," Cristian continues. "I spent more time with him and I actually listened to him and got to know him. I can see how he might give off an egoistic first impression, sure, but underneath, he's a really kind person."

My ears are burning. "Are you fucking kidding me? I'm asking you to stop seeing him because the guy is deranged and potentially dangerous and you're coming back at me with, 'he's a really kind person'?"

Cristian sighs. "I'm not invalidating your experience with him. I'm just telling you mine. You don't know for sure that it was him who catfished you."

I stay silent. Because the truth is, outside of my gut feeling, I really don't.

Fork clanks against metal as Cristian scrapes the contents of the frying pan onto two plates. "And we both know you have a tendency to overreact and exaggerate whenever you're faced with a new challenge. And remember how jealous you were when I first started hanging out with Danny? And you've never even met him."

I scoff in disbelief. "Have I ever asked you to stop seeing anyone before? No."

"No," Cristian agrees. "But you've also never met any of the men I've dated before either. And this is *exactly* why I've never wanted to introduce them to you. I knew it would only lead to jealousy."

"Jesus Christ," I say. "I'm not jealous! I'm *worried* about you!"

"And I appreciate that, mi amor," Cristian says, still calm. "I'll keep my guard up. But I can take care of myself. I'll stop seeing Russell soon, I promise. I have to anyway. But I can't just cut people off. You know that."

I feel a surge of anger. "Does Russell *fuck* you that good?"

Cristian whips his face my way, his nostrils flaring. "You know what, Greg? Sometimes, it disgusts me how obsessed with sex you are. And it's only gotten worse these past few months." He swipes a plate of stir-fry and carries it over to the sofa.

My face sears. "Sure, deflect the question, why not."

Eyes on his food, Cristian says, under his nose, "Increíble. I can't believe how two men with such similar upbringings can be so different."

"Similar upbringings?"

"For your information," he goes on, glaring at me, "unlike you, Russell doesn't just fuck anything that moves. To him, sex actually means something."

The tips of my nails dig deeper into my palms. "Oh yeah?" I say. "In that case, maybe you should be married and raising children with him."

Not waiting for Cristian to reply, I march over to the bedroom, where I shut the door and text Elijah. *Miss you*, I write and hit send. I fall back on the bed, my arms over my head. I close my eyes and exhale a long breath.

While I wait for Elijah to respond, a strange feeling starts burrowing itself into my gut. What did Cristian mean by *two men with such similar upbringings*? Sure, Russell and I are the same age but…

I sit straight up, my heart pounding. Grabbing my phone, I dial my mom's number and bring it up to my ear.

"Now this is a surprise," she says.

"Hi, Mom. I need you to do something for me."

A sigh. "Of course you do. Why else would you be calling?

You haven't even talked to me since your cousin's wedding."

"Huh? We text all the time."

"It's not the same."

"Mom, I need you to look at my yearbook from, like, fourth grade."

"I'm watching a cooking competition show with your father right now."

"Mom, *please*. This is important."

"Can't it wait until tomorrow? The yearbooks are upstairs."

"No, it can't! Please!"

She lets out a long groan. I hear shuffling. "Can you pause it?" My dad's muffled voice in the background. "…wants me to look at his yearbook." I pinch my thigh in frustration. "Yes, right now…no, didn't tell me."

"Mom!"

More shuffling. "Is the baby okay?" she asks.

"Yes."

"Did you get the package?"

"What package?"

"The toys."

"Not yet."

"Really? It should've gotten there by now. Let me know when you get it."

"I will." After a beat, I add, "Thanks."

She starts heaving, which means she's reached the stairs. "And how's Cristian?"

"He's fine."

"Your father and I are fine too, by the way, thank you for asking."

"Mom, we just texted, like, three days ago."

"Your brother stopped by earlier. Of course he needed something, too…" She keeps talking but I'm not really listening. My mind is somewhere else entirely. Somewhere far in the past, to be exact.

Finally, I hear the squeak of the closet door.

"What grade did you say?" she asks.

"Check fourth first."

"What am I looking for exactly?"

"I want you to look under the M's for the last name Mailey."

"I wish I brought my glasses…"

"Ugh! You didn't bring your glasses?"

"It's fine, I can see." The thumps of books being rearranged. "The one from St. Vincent, right?"

"Yeah…"

As she turns the pages—I can hear the rustling of paper—she starts talking about my sister-in-law but I'm not paying attention. I'm just willing her to move faster.

"What name did you say?" she asks.

"Mailey."

"I don't see it…"

"Because you don't have your glasses on or because he's not in there?"

A tsk. "Because he's not in here. I checked all the M's for all classes."

"Can you check the book from fifth grade?"

After some more shuffling and slapping, and some more low-key shit-talking about my sister-in-law, my mom starts spelling the name out loud.

"M-A-I-L-E-Y, yes?"

"Correct."

"Russell Mailey," she says.

A chill skids over my skin. "Really?"

"Right here next to Amy Marks. Is this who you were looking for? Who is he?"

"Thanks, Mom. I'll call you tomorrow."

I hang up and stare at the wall. My heart is thundering in my chest, like a thrashing animal too big for its cage. But I also feel oddly numb. I'm somehow unable to fully process this new information. It's as if it's too ridiculous, too outlandish to be true. I already knew Russell was not right in the head, but this? This implies a much more profound level of lunacy than I could've imagined.

The first time I went out with Russell Mailey on a date, when, after a sip of his whiskey he told me his full name, I assumed it sounded familiar to me because he's famous. But that wasn't it. I don't know any fucking producers, save for maybe two or three super famous ones. Russell's fame had nothing to do with it. The reason his name sounded familiar to me was because *I had already met him.*

In school.

Do you want to kiss me?

Russell Mailey went to the same Catholic school I did.

Russell Mailey is the first boy I ever kissed. The boy from the school bathroom.

Rocketing to my feet, I swing open the bedroom door and march into the living room. Cristian's on the sofa, his finished plate sitting beside his open laptop on the coffee table. His lenses reflect the light from the screen. He doesn't look up. The plate of stir-fry he made for me, covered by a film of plastic, sits on the kitchen counter.

"So I just called my mom," I announce, my voice quivering. His eyes briefly flick up. "Mmhm," he says.

"I had weird feeling in my gut so I asked her to check my old yearbooks, from Catholic school."

"Okay."

I pause for effect. "Russell went to fifth grade with me."

Cristian looks up and glares. "Yes, I *know*."

My heart shoots up to my throat. "You know?"

"You *don't*?" he asks, accusingly. "Jesus. Russell said you were unimpressed when he told you, but it turns out you weren't even paying fucking attention. The reason he swiped right on you on Tinder in the first place was because he recognized you."

"He never told me that!" I counter. "He lied to me. He said he was from New Jersey." Even as I say this, though, I'm not convinced that's entirely true. Did Russell ever say anything about living in Chicago? He might have…

"No," Cristian says, "He lived in Chicago before he lived in New Jersey. See? This is what I was talking about. You know nothing about the man."

"He never told me that…"

"Maybe you were just too busy thinking about his ass to hear it."

My face burns because, yes, it's possible that instead of listening to Russell's droning, I was thinking about his ass. But no. I wouldn't miss something as significant as him telling me that we went to the same school as kids.

"Remember that story I told you about my first kiss?" I go on. "About that kid who was staring at me in the bathroom? The one I asked if he wanted to kiss me? Well, guess what? That kid was Russell Fucking Mailey."

Behind his thick glasses, Cristian rolls his eyes.

"It was him. I'm one-hundred percent sure. He didn't tell you that part, did he?"

"No, he didn't."

"Well, the guy clearly has some kind of obsession with me."

"Obsession?" Cristian laughs. "Greg, por favor. Russell is a famous, successful man. Even if he did kiss you when you were ten, you think he has time to dig up old flings? And from fifth grade? You're being ridiculous."

"*I'm* ridiculous? How can you not see how *creepy* this whole thing is?"

"What's creepy is how jealous and obsessed *you* are about this. You always do this kind of stuff whenever a big change is looming. Obsess over little things and make a big deal out of nothing. You promise me it'll be okay and then you act like this anyway. It's all just in your head, mi amor."

"It's not," I protest, but my voice is weak.

Cristian's jaw tightens. "If anything, you should be focusing on how *you* treated *Russell*. You didn't listen to him when he talked and you used him for sex. How is that okay?" He pauses, making sure his words sink in. "Let him be."

Stupefied by his indictment of the situation, I stare at him. Quietly, I say, "You're wrong. This time it's different." I turn and start toward the bedroom, leaving the plate Cristian had prepared for me sitting, cold and untouched, on the counter.

CHAPTER 22

I know I'm a great kisser but, for fuck's sake, we were in fifth grade, I write in a text. *You're even more pathetic and disturbed than I thought.*

Russell doesn't respond.

Kate, when I vent to her about my discovery in another text, is maybe even more creeped-out than I am. *Ew! Stop! I can't!* she writes. *That is TOO WILD!*

I'm not sure what to do, I say. *Any advice?*

Hmm. Do you think there's a chance Russell did tell you about the school thing and you just missed it?

I take a deep breath. *I don't even know anymore...*

Cristian's smart, she says. *I'm sure he knows what he's doing. You've conveyed to him how important this is to you. I'm sure he'll stop seeing the guy.*

I fucking hope so.

For the next few days, things remain a bit tense, you could say, between my husband and me. Not to the point where our routine is disrupted, but there's definitely a charged undercur-

161

rent beneath our interactions. The whole time I feel like Cristian's just waiting for Russell's name to slip out of my mouth again.

Well, it doesn't. I make it my mission not to bring up Russell again and I stick to it. Cristian is my husband. I trust him. And, after what I told him, I trust him to make the right decision. Which is to stop seeing that creepy fucker sooner rather than later.

On Thursday, when I get home from a quickie at Elijah's, Cristian surprises me with a rich, homemade seafood paella. The mouth-watering aroma of shrimp, garlic, and lemon thaws away most of my annoyance with Cristian over Russell. I decide to let it go, for now at least, especially since tomorrow night is Kate's birthday and I'm looking forward to going with Cristian on my arm as usual.

"Smells delicious," I say.

"Thanks," he says, setting up the table.

Once we're both sitting at it, our steaming plates in front of us, I decide to bestow my official peace-offering: "Do you want to grab dinner together somewhere before we head over to the party tomorrow?"

Cristian lowers his fork and looks at me. "What party?" he asks.

"Um. Kate's birthday party?"

Cristian's eyes briefly widen before he winces, as if in pain. He crumples, his head sagging forward. "Joder," he says. "I completely forgot."

"Well, now you remember."

The pain on his face seems to intensify and, with it, so does my unease. "Greg," he says, his thick eyebrows in a knot. "I don't think I can go."

At this, I actually laugh. "What do you mean you can't go?" I ask. The party's not negotiable. It's Kate's thirtieth. He has to go. *We* have to go. Together.

"I made other plans on accident," he says. "I'm sorry."

"So cancel them."

A plea forms in his eyes. "I *can't.*"

"Cristian," I say, dread building at the base of my stomach. "What are you talking about? You knew about Kate's birthday party for *months.* It's her *thirtieth.*"

"I know, I completely forgot. I'll make it up to her. Maybe I can even stop by after my thing. I'm not sure what time it's going to end."

"What last-minute plans could possibly be more important than going to your good friend's birthday party with your fucking husband?"

Cristian takes a deep breath. "It's an awards ceremony…"

For a second, I'm confused. "What awards ceremony?"

Cristian's voice gets smaller. "For TV creators," he answers.

While the dots connect in my head, I hold my breath. Then I release it with a cackle. A loud, no-holds-barred cackle. "Seriously? *Russell?*"

Cristian drops his gaze to his untouched meal. "He doesn't have anyone else to go with. And he's nominated…"

"Who the fuck cares!"

"I promised him I'd go with him a week ago. I was going to tell you sooner but things have already been so tense…"

I clench my teeth. "Cancel on him."

"I can't."

"Cristian, *cancel* on him."

"I can't! He needs me to go with him."

"Listen to yourself!" I yell. "*I* need you! I'm your husband and I'm asking you to go with *me*. Are you saying that creepy asshole is more important to you than I am?"

Cristian lets out a tsk. "Obviously, you are more important. But it's a monumental event in his life. And the anniversary of his father's death is coming up and he's broken up about it. I know what that can feel like. I lost my father too. Por favor, Greg, *please* understand. I fucked up, I know. But it's just a party. I'll call Kate and explain."

A rush of adrenaline sweeps through me. Without a word, I set my fork on the table and get up.

"Where are you going?" he asks, panic weaving into his voice.

"Out," I say.

By the door, as I'm tying my shoes, Cristian comes to hover over me, arms crossed. "Come on, Greg, where are you going? It's late," he's saying, but I pretend not to hear him. I grab my keys and shut the door behind me.

Outside, my skin tingling, I breathe in the warm night air. While I wait for the car I ordered to arrive, I pace around in a circle. A Yorkshire terrier on a leash pulls a woman in yoga pants in my direction. The two are illuminated by the yellow light from a streetlamp. "Evening," I say a little too eagerly when they pass. Without a word, the woman speeds up, taking the helm from the dog.

When I get to my destination, I search for the apartment number on the digital intercom. A screen reflects my own face back at me.

"Yeah?" I hear crackling through the speaker. I recognize the voice. It's Brian—the introverted straight roommate I've met once or twice.

"Hey, it's Greg," I say, even though I know he can see me on camera. "I'm here for Elijah. Can you let me up?"

There's a stretch of silence.

"Hello?" I say.

"Hey," Brian says. Another pause. "Um, hold on."

"Oh. Sure." I straighten and plunge my hands into my pockets. I turn around and pretend to be fascinated by the wine store across the street.

"Hello?"

I whirl around. "Yeah?"

"Elijah's not here, sorry."

Disappointment punches me in the gut. "Is he coming back soon?"

"I don't know."

"Did he, like, step out for a minute? Or has he been gone for a while?"

"I really don't know, man, sorry."

"Oh, okay, no worries. Thanks."

I take a deep breath. Earlier today, when Elijah and I had our little tryst, did he mention having any plans for tonight? I don't think so. He's probably just at the grocery store.

Nearby, I spot a knee-high tree guard enclosing a young maple. I shuffle over, and, since I don't have a better idea, I sit on top of it and wait.

Ten minutes later, my ass getting numb from the iron rod, I pull out my phone and open Instagram. Immediately, I notice that Elijah has uploaded a new story. My pulse quickens. Of course. Why didn't I check Instagram before?

Elijah's first upload shows a photo of a large, round plate. Its edges are spotted with a ring of colorful piles of meats and vegetables. Between these piles are the instantly recognizable rolls of Ethiopian flatbread, injera.

Okay, so Elijah's at dinner.

The next segment is a selfie. Elijah's holding a piece of the distinct, gray-colored bread topped with a heavy dose of veggie wot. My heart flutters at how kissable he looks. The need to see him swells up within me.

The third upload is a video. It's a sweeping shot of the tabletop. Towards the end of the clip, the camera moves up from the dishes and points to the other end of the table, revealing the person Elijah is with, because, it turns out, Elijah's not alone.

A cold shudder passes over my skin.

Wait. *What?*

Chapter 23

Numbed and confused, I replay the video once, twice.

On the third time, I raise the volume. Elijah's voice reaches my ears. "How's the food, mister?" he asks. I play the clip again. "How's the food, mister?" And again: "How's the food, mister?" It sounds like Elijah is speaking through a smile.

Every time, the video ends with Russell's smirk and his thumb spiked upwards in approval. And with that deliberate fix of his eyes on the lens of the camera that feels like it's meant just for me, like he knew I'd be watching.

I notice how shallow my breaths have gotten. Suddenly, there's not enough air in New York City. I shoot up to my feet.

Fumbling with my phone, I replay the video one final time. I note the timestamp and the name of the restaurant. The video went public forty-three minutes ago. The restaurant, I see, is in Murray Hill. I could jump in an Uber and rush over. But forty-three minutes is a good chunk of time. I'd get there and they could be long gone.

I decide to stay put and wait. It's a weeknight. Elijah's bound to come home at some point. But Russell does have a comfy, king-sized bed. And he does live alone.

Hey, I say in the text I furiously compose, *I'm in your neighborhood. Need to talk.* I'm sweating from every pore. I have an urge to call Cristian. If I ever needed more evidence to prove that Russell's a psychopath, this is it. But then I remember how I stormed out, leaving Cristian alone in our apartment.

Maybe Elijah and Russell have a mutual friend—who was even there, in the restaurant with them, just out of shot of Elijah's camera. There might be another explanation. But even as I'm coming up with these excuses I know this is no coincidence in the same way I knew that Russell meeting Cristian was no coincidence, either.

But once is bad enough. Doing this to me *twice*?

One moment, I want to cry, like a child, bullied. The next, I'm gritting my teeth, imagining tackling Russell to the sidewalk and repeatedly kicking his face into the pavement with the heel of my shoe.

The doors of Elijah's building swing open and Brian—Elijah's roommate, the one I had the intercom conversation with earlier—comes out in gym shorts and flip-flops. After a double take, he recognizes me and gives me a wary nod. When I nod back, I try to make myself look less like a stalker by forcing a smile.

I sit back down on my tree guard and think. When Elijah gets here, I can't act too paranoid, too angry. I made that mistake with Cristian. If I rush up to him demanding answers, he'll think I'm jealous, crazy, or both. Objectively, I can see how that would be a major turn off, especially after a nice dinner. And, considering what a charming gentleman Russell can pretend to be, it probably was a nice dinner.

When I imagine Russell having sex with Elijah, bile climbs my throat. It makes me sick and furious at the same time. With Cristian, it was easier. Cristian's mature. He's an adult. When I picture Russell fucking Elijah, *soiling* him, I want to scream.

A shape appears down the block. Instantly, I recognize it as Elijah. He's alone. My chest loosens with relief. I shoot up to my feet. The moment Elijah realizes I'm the guy loitering in front of his building, his face sets into a puzzled expression.

"Hi," I say.

"Hey," he replies, cautiously. "Sorry, um, I just saw your text." He briefly cuts eye contact, which means he's probably lying, but it doesn't matter. So he didn't reply to me right away. Not a big deal.

"All good," I say and lean over to kiss him. Moments ago, were Russell's lips on his lips too? The thought makes me nauseous. "Can we talk?"

"Um..." He shoots a glance up the wall of his building, as if considering whether to invite me upstairs, like I hope he will. But I guess he decides against it because he adds, "Sure. Want to go to our bar?"

At that, my heart warms a bit. *Our* bar. "Perfect," I reply.

As we fall into step together, Elijah asks, "So what's this about?" There's a hint of accusation in his voice, but again, it's totally understandable given the circumstances. "You're making me kind of nervous here." He tries to laugh.

I tighten my grip around his hand. "I saw your Instagram story."

He stiffens, slowing. "Okay..."

I stop walking altogether. "How do you know Russell Mailey?" I ask.

With our hands still linked, Elijah has to stop, too. A small frown forms on his face. He shrugs. "I don't know, I met him on one of the apps, I guess."

"When?"

A flicker of annoyance. "A while ago. Why?"

"What's a while ago?"

"A couple of weeks ago."

"Was it before you met me or after?"

"After. *Why*?"

I nod to myself, unsurprised.

"Will you tell me what this is about or not?" he asks.

"I went out on a few dates with him before I met you."

Elijah's expression shifts from annoyance to curiosity. "You did?"

"Yeah. We had sex, too, obviously."

"Huh..." he says. "That's kind of hot, actually..."

I wince at the comment but ignore it. "Technically, I've known him since fifth grade. Remember that story I told you about my first kiss in Catholic school?"

Elijah's eyebrows hike up. "No way."

"That was my reaction when I found out, too," I say. "But it was him, I'm sure of it. He must've sought me out or something, I don't know. Anyway, after we hooked up, we didn't end things on the best note. He cried and everything."

"Russell *cried*?"

"Sure did. I didn't hear from him for a while after that until he called me to ask for another chance. When I said no, he basically admitted that he had catfished me in the past and told me that I'm not fit to be a father."

"What?" Elijah chuckles, awkwardly.

"I thought that was the end of it but I was wrong," I go on. "One night—remember when you canceled on our movie plans?" Elijah nods, momentarily averts his gaze. "Well, that night, I came home to find him in my house."

"What do you mean?"

I realize we're blocking the sidewalk so I let go of Elijah's hand and allow a woman to pass between us. "He was hooking up with Cristian."

Elijah just stares at me.

"They claimed it was a coincidence but I knew better. The following day, I talked to Russell, one on one, and, just as I suspected, he confirmed to me that it wasn't." Yes, I'm simplifying and slightly changing what actually happened but, for all intents and purposes, I'm not lying. "He's sleeping with Cristian to get back at me."

A glint of skepticism forms in Elijah's eye but I press on, even though it doesn't need to be said. "And now," I say, "he's sleeping with you."

Elijah's head rolls back.

"What?" I ask.

"That all sounds very...*extra*," he says.

"Yeah," I say. "It is. It's *fucked up*."

"Are you sure we're talking about the same Russell?"

"Positive."

"And *why* would he do this exactly?"

I shrug. "I don't know. Because he's deeply disturbed?"

Elijah chuckles, his head tilting. "Greg, come on."

"Come on *what*?"

"Russell's, like, the biggest gentleman."

My face explodes with heat. "No, he's not. He's a liar and a fake," I say, doing my best to maintain composure. "He's only charming when he needs to be."

Elijah shrugs. "I don't know…He's been nothing but genuine with me." He throws a glance back toward his building. "Do you want to just get ice cream, instead?" he asks. "I don't really want to stay out too late. I'm kind of tired."

"Are you *listening* to me?"

"Of course."

"You're acting like you don't care."

"What do you want me to say? It's unusual but, I mean, what do you expect? That's the gay community for you. Sure, we live in New York, but still. There aren't *that* many of us. We're still a minority. It's bound to get a little incestuous."

I'm stunned. "You can't be serious."

"And, honestly," he goes on, "I really can't picture Russell doing any of that stuff. I'll talk to him. I'm sure there's an explanation."

I feel sick. "You're going to see him again?"

"Yeah, why wouldn't I?"

"You have to stay away from him. Who knows what he's capable of?"

Elijah lets out a sigh. "Look, Greg," he says. "I get that you're a little upset. But I'm allowed to see other guys. Even if they're someone you know."

I huff. "You think I'm just jealous?"

Elijah doesn't answer but the way he shrugs makes it clear that he does. "I'm not exactly thrilled about you sleeping next to Cristian every night either," he says. "But that's the way it is. I'll talk to Russell, okay? Find out what's going on."

My ears, my neck, everything feels like it's burning. With everything I got, I fight the urge to give Elijah an ultimatum: *It's either him or me. You have to choose.* The words are there at the tip of my tongue. But I keep them to myself. I'm too angry right now. And too scared of what he might say.

So, instead, I plant a short but intense kiss on his lips and say, "I think I'll pass on the ice cream tonight."

"Greg…"

"Goodnight, cute stuff." I turn away. Behind me, I hear him repeat my name, but, as much as I want to, I don't turn around.

CHAPTER 24

I'm awakened by someone's attempt to wriggle out of my grip. Almost instantly, because of the familiar smell and shape, I recognize this someone as my husband. We're in our bed and I'm spooning Cristian from behind.

Once I register that he just wants to get ready for work, I release him. The moment I do, my head explodes with pricks of sharp pain.

The events of last night come swimming back to me. My fight with Cristian. Seeing Elijah. Getting out of a cab in front of Russell's place. Arguing with the concierge, who kept insisting Russell wasn't home, and marching toward the elevators anyway. Pounding my fists on Russell's door until I was escorted out of the building.

All the Negronis and vodka sodas I downed after. The short, black-haired Greenpoint boy with the blanket, whom I followed up the stairwell all the way to the roof because he couldn't host me in his room. The thick, frothy darkness of the night. The Manhattan skyline, shimmering.

"What time is it?" I grumble, rubbing my fists into my eyes.

"It's already seven thirty," Cristian says. "Good morning."

His words contain a heavy dose of disappointment but they also include a lot of love. A wave of shame washes over me. "Good morning," I reply.

"Someone had quite a night," he says.

I muster the courage to look up at him. There's a solemn expression on his face, the reasons behind it hanging in the air between us. "I'm sorry about last night, mi amor," I say. "I shouldn't have gotten that angry."

He sighs. "I'm sorry too."

I smile at him and he smiles back. I'm flooded with so much relief that, for a few seconds, my headache is completely cured.

"Shouldn't you be getting ready for work?" he asks.

"I think I'm going to call in sick today."

Cristian nods and leaves the room. He returns with a glass of water and an aspirin. My head throbs extra hard as I gratefully down both. I'm even more grateful for the kiss Cristian gives me afterwards. It's slightly more tepid than usual but it's a kiss, nonetheless. "Okay," he says. "I guess I'll see you later tonight then." He hesitates, like he wants to say more. But he doesn't. He doesn't mention Kate's birthday party.

"Okay," I reply. "Have a good day at work." I don't bring up Russell's award ceremony, which Cristian's set to attend tonight, either. More importantly, I don't tell him what I found out about Russell and Elijah. The urge is there, and the thought of Cristian spending the evening with Russell makes my stomach churn, but, for now, I decide to stay quiet. I'll tell him later. I don't want to risk another fight. Besides, if all goes as planned, Cristian won't be seeing Russell tonight anyway.

As soon as my husband shuts the front door behind him, I slip out of bed and get ready for the day myself. I take my time. There's no need to hurry because I have until lunchtime and the train ride to SoHo won't take very long.

Last night, Russell might've been a coward, pretending not to be home—and maybe rightfully so; I would've smashed my fist into his face—but today, we'll be in public, near his workplace. He'll have no choice but to hear me out.

When I'm showered, caffeinated, and content with the various details of my mission, I get on my phone. I scroll through Russell's Instagram account, read his Wikipedia page, watch a few interviews, and scan a bunch of articles about the TV shows he was involved in in the past and the TV shows he has in the pipeline for the future—some of which I recall hearing about from him directly. I also find a few mentions of his nomination in tonight's ceremony. God, I hope the motherfucker doesn't win.

When eleven o'clock rolls around, armed with the address of Russell's production company in SoHo and the determination to end this little game of his today no matter what, I leave the house.

In SoHo, people wander in and out of brand-name stores, wait in line for gelato. The tourists are easy to spot. They have shopping bags and give off a general vibe of either trying too hard or not hard enough. The locals are much more elegant, unflappable. I've always liked the area, especially the cobblestone streets, and I've always envied the wealthy New Yorkers who get to live in the spacious lofts overlooking them—some of which I've had the chance to see from the inside thanks to a Grindr rendezvous or two.

Passing an upscale gym, I make eye contact with a lean, square-jawed runway model type who steps out through the door. He smiles at me but I trudge past. If this were happening under different circumstances, I would make a beeline for him and offer to buy him a coffee. The guy's gorgeous. Probably Eastern European—Ukrainian, maybe—temporarily brought over to the city by his big shot modeling agency. But, today, seconds after he's out of my field of vision, I forget all about him.

Diagonally across the street from Russell's office, I luck out and find a bar counter seat at a packed Mediterranean restaurant. From my stool, I have the entrance to Russell's building in full view. Perfect. I also know I couldn't have missed him because it's only noon and I have the cringe-worthy memory of him telling me about his "permanent one o'clock lunch reservations" at all the best restaurants downtown.

As I wait, though, I develop an itch of worry that Russell might not even be around today, that he might be at a shoot upstate somewhere—or hell, even in LA. But I remind myself that he was just with Elijah the night before, and he's going to— or he *thinks* he's going to—his precious award ceremony with Cristian tonight.

Sure enough, when the clock hits 12:45 p.m., I see him.

Instantly, my body releases a gush of sweat. And instantly, I'm sliding off my stool, leaving my already-paid-for vodka soda on the counter.

With Russell locked in my sight the whole time, I weave way my through the restaurant and out onto the sidewalk, where I almost collide with a group of Italians. "Sorry," I mumble and dash past their grimaced faces and into the street.

Russell's in his usual slick producer attire. Dress pants and a white collared shirt, top two buttons unbuttoned. He moves with purpose. He looks important. Accompanying him are two other men, one my age, one younger.

I arrive on their side of the street just as they're walking past.

"Russell?" I call with pretend surprise.

Russell's lips stop moving. His face tenses—but only for a second. Once he realizes who he's dealing with, it relaxes, almost to the point of boredom. This is disappointing, as I was hoping to rattle him.

"Greg," he says, his mouth forming into a tight smile.

"I saw you from across the street," I say, purely for the benefit of the two men he's with. "I thought I'd say hi. Come have lunch with me."

Russell's staring at me. "I'm actually on the way to eat with these two lovely gentlemen," he says, indicating each of his companions in turn.

"Come have lunch with me," I repeat more slowly, less nicely.

If Russell feels threatened, he doesn't show it. Like a parent giving in to a petulant child, he sighs and turns to the older of his two coworkers. "Sorry," he says. "I'll catch up with you guys in a bit."

"Huh?" the older guy says. "You're kidding, right?"

"This won't take long."

"What the fuck, Russell. The Swedes need an answer by two!"

To this, Russell doesn't even reply. He steps away from the men and urges me to follow. "I thought I might be running into you," he tells me as we start in the opposite direction of where he was previously going. "Sorry I missed you last night."

"All good," I say. "I would've been scared, too."

Russell laughs. "I was out."

"Sure you were."

"It was Elijah's Instagram story, wasn't it?" he asks. I don't even have to look at him to know that he's got a smirk on his face. "Nice touch, right? My idea."

Slamming my palm into Russell's shoulder, I send him stumbling into the window of a boutique shoe store. I want to do more but my move draws a lot of eyes. From Russell, however, it only draws more laughter. "Careful," he says, brushing off his shoulder as if my hand had left a stain. "You don't want to get yourself in trouble."

"Stay the fuck away from him."

Russell's grin doesn't waver. "Why should I? Aren't *you* the one who has to stay the fuck away from him soon?"

Dashing up to him, I park my face an inch away from his beard. "Last time we talked I asked you to fuck off nicely. You didn't listen."

"No," he says, his coffee breath hitting my lips. "I didn't."

"Everything all right here?" I hear in a booming, Southern accent. I turn to find a middle-aged man—stocky, ex-military vibes—standing nearby.

"Absolutely," Russell answers, smiling at him, then aiming that annoying smile at me. This only stirs my anger further.

"Stay the fuck away from Elijah," I hiss. "*And* Cristian."

"So greedy!" Russell exclaims with a laugh. "Does Cristian know how much you like Elijah? How protective you are of him? Is that even allowed in your little arrangement?"

I have an urge to launch my forehead into his face and break his nose. "Do you hear me? Stay the fuck away from them or—"

"Or *what*, Greg?" he interrupts, his blue eyes piercing mine.

I clench down on my teeth. He's right. Or what? My plan was to scare him, but he's not. Not even a little. If anything, he's enjoying this.

I inch closer.

"Hey!" the stocky dude warns.

"It's fine," Russell says to the man. "I got this."

At my side, my fist twitches. Never before have I wanted to physically injure a person as much as I do right now. For a few seconds, I genuinely consider it. Getting arrested might actually be worth the pleasure it'd bring.

Russell says, "You brought this on yourself."

"Did I now?" I challenge.

"Absolutely. What goes around comes around. Didn't they teach you that in school? They must have. We did go to the same one."

"What the *fuck* is wrong with you?" I shout. "Don't you have anything better to do with your time? What did you even expect? Hmm? That you'd dig up the boy who kissed you in fifth grade, go out with him on a date and what? Live happily ever after?"

Russell shrugs. "I told you," he says, smugly. "I believe in fate."

"Well, guess what," I growl. "We're not meant to be."

"And maybe," he says, "you're not meant to be with Cristian or Elijah."

I glance around. The ex-military man is gone, as is our audience. "I'm going to say this one last time. Stay away from them or I'll kill you."

At this, Russell laughs the hardest yet.

Spitting on someone without his or her consent is considered assault. I know this, I'm aware of it, and yet, in this moment, I can't restrain myself. I snap my head back and launch a wad of saliva right into the middle of Russell's face.

Russell brings up a hand. "That's not very nice," he says, wiping the spit off with his fingers. He turns away, but then halts again. "Wish me luck at the awards ceremony tonight." He shoots me a wink. "I'll say hi to Cristian for you."

CHAPTER 25

From SoHo, I jump back on the M train and cross over to Brooklyn. I consider texting or maybe even calling Cristian to tell him about what just transpired with Russell, but I have a feeling he'll take me more seriously in person. Since Williamsburg is on the way home anyway, I decide to pay him a visit at work.

He's not too happy about it.

I already had my lunch break, he texts back after I inform him that I'll be arriving in front of his studio in approximately three minutes.

It's important, I reply. *Just come out for a bit.*

He makes me wait for almost half an hour before he does. "Sorry," he mumbles, wiping his forehead with the back of his hand. Colorful splotches of paint stain his charcoal-colored coveralls. "What's wrong?"

"It's Russell," I say.

At the name, Cristian's lips turn downward. "You couldn't text me?"

"No," I say. "Listen. He's been seeing *Elijah*, too."

"So?"

"*So?*"

"Joder." Cristian is massaging his temple. "Who gives a shit? He's a free man."

"You don't think that's *strange*? First you, then another guy I'm seeing?"

"No, Greg, I don't. And I'm at work." He indicates his coveralls with a sweep of his arms. "Can we talk about this after the awards ceremony tonight?"

"No. I don't want you to go that ceremony with him."

His expression hardens. "This? Again?"

"Promise me you won't go," I say. "Come to Kate's party with me. You know I wouldn't be asking if it wasn't important. Please, mi amor. Do it for me."

Cristian turns his face to the side and scoffs. His head shakes a few times. "I'm going back to work," he says and starts walking away.

I don't stop him. I know that, to Cristian, my request might seem unreasonable. Jealous, possessive, paranoid, whatever. It'll probably put another damper on our relationship. But I don't regret making it. Cristian may not see Russell for who he really is, but I do. My husband's just going to have to trust me on this one.

Even though he didn't specifically make the promise, Cristian does end up coming to Kate's party with me. He cancels on Russell and he joins me instead. He chooses me. Because he loves *me*. And Russell can go fuck himself.

"Hey, you two," Kate says, shuffling over to where Cristian and I are sulking in the corner of her apartment. The thin-strap dress she's wearing shows off her beautiful, toned shoulders. She's a perceptive one so I'm sure she can tell something's up. Since we arrived, we've only done the bare minimum amount of mingling. Not only with her and her guests but with each other, too. "You good?"

I tried talking to Cristian, making conversation as usual, but all I got in return was one-word responses. Again, I get it. He has a right to be pissed. He could've been socializing with celebrities tonight. Instead, he's here with me.

To appease Kate, and because he's a sweetheart, Cristian whips out his infectious smile, the areas under his eyes crinkling in that inviting way I envy and love. He raises his glass of wine. "Yes, of course," he says "Salud, mami. Happy birthday."

Taking Cristian's lead, I smile and clink my own wine glass with theirs. Kate's boyfriend, Hiro, appears and adds a fourth glass to the mix. More clinks. "Relationship goals," he says, nodding to Cristian and me. At the comment, Cristian snorts.

"Uh-oh," Hiro says, picking up on the vibe. "Trouble in paradise?" Kate jabs him in the gut with her elbow. He buckles over. "What the fuck, Kate?"

While this is happening, Cristian chugs the rest of his wine. "All right," he says. "I'm ready for some real alcohol. Who's with me?"

Hiro tips the remainder of his own wine into his mouth, raises a hand, and follows Cristian over to the makeshift bar in kitchen.

Kate shuffles closer to me. "What's going on?" she asks.

I sigh. "I don't want to bore you with our problems. It's your birthday."

"Are you kidding?" she says. "I just spent fifteen minutes

listening to Angelica talk about her cacti. Spill it."

Drawing a deep breath, I say, "It's Russell…"

She nods. "Is Cristian still seeing him?"

"Yeah. But guess what? Elijah is seeing him now too."

Her jaw drops. "WHAT?"

"Kate," I say, my voice shaky. I realize, for the first time, how unnerved about the situation I really am. "The guy is seriously fucked in the head."

"How does he know Elijah?"

I shrug. "Elijah said they met on Tinder or some other app."

"You think Russell sought him out on there?"

"I *know* he sought him out on there."

"Man," she says, "that is creepy as hell."

"Tell me about it. I confronted him again today. I threatened to kill him and spat in his face and everything. And, Kate, he didn't even flinch. I think he's trying to punish me or teach me a lesson or something."

"What? Get the fuck out," she says. "Does this guy think he's living in one of his TV shows or something?"

"Who the fuck knows."

Her concerned eyes roll over my face. "Well, he *is* harassing you and stuff. Can't you get the police involved?"

I let out a manufactured laugh. "And say what? Officer, this guy is involved with both my husband and my lover?" I shake my head. "If anything, I'm the one who could get in trouble. I technically assaulted him today."

Kate thinks for a moment. "You told Cristian about this, right?"

"Yeah."

"And?"

I exhale. "And Cristian thinks that it's all a coincidence and that I'm jealous and paranoid and making a big deal out of nothing like I always do."

"Oh, honey," she says, but before she can say anything else, her younger sister, Serena, invades our little corner. "Sis!" she says. "Get over here." Smiling a tight "sorry" smile at me, she grabs Kate by the arm and starts pulling her away.

While she's being hauled off, Kate looks back at me and says, "Forget about all that shit tonight. Have fun. Go get a stronger drink with Hiro!"

I blow her an air kiss and, taking a sip of my wine, search the room for my husband. At the other end, past a bunch of people, I spot him leaning against the wall with Hiro, who looks extremely fascinated by whatever Cristian is gesticulating.

Turning my back to them, I pull out my phone and pop open Instagram. Right away, my pulse quickens. Elijah has posted a new story. I tap it.

First, I see a panoramic shot of a party. There are suits and gowns, cameras and beautiful smiles. Next, there's a photo of Elijah in a suit of his own, standing next to an actress I vaguely recognize from an HBO show. In the background, I can see an elegant banquet hall. Finally, there's a selfie of Elijah at a fancy table.

With Russell sitting at his side.

I grind my teeth. In a way, I'm not surprised. Of course this is a move Russell would pull. *Of course* he'd take Elijah to the awards ceremony instead of Cristian.

Phone in hand, I march across the room towards my husband. Sliding up beside him, I raise the phone to his face. "Look," I say. "See how much of a psycho your Russell is? This is why I want you to stop seeing him."

Cristian glances at the screen, then at me. "I'm talking to Hiro," he says.

"See how disposable you are to him? See how conniving he is?"

"Greg, I'm in the middle of a conversation."

"This is Elijah. Look."

Cristian lets out a *tsk*. "I'm sorry," he says to Hiro. "I'll be right back." Hiro nods and Cristian begins walking away. I follow him past the balcony—packed to the brim with people smoking—until we're both in Kate's bathroom. "Joder," he grunts, shutting the two of us inside. "You know I hate arguing in public."

"Who's arguing?"

"You are! Why are you so worked up?"

"I have a reason to be! Don't you see what Russell's doing?"

"*What* is he doing?"

"He took Elijah to the awards ceremony!"

"So? He had to take someone since *I* was not allowed to go with him, no?"

"Are you fucking kidding me? You seriously don't think this is fucked up?"

"No! Dios mío, *why* do you care so much? You're obsessing over the silliest things again. *What* are you so worried about?"

"He's doing this to get under my skin." I raise my phone again, as if showing him the photo of Russell and Elijah one more time will somehow change his mind.

"But why does it get under your skin?" Cristian asks. "Hmm? Why does it matter to you what Russell does?" His expression darkens. "Or is this more about Elijah?" He pauses. "Elijah's free to do whatever he wants as well, no? Don't you agree? He's just your temporary fuck-buddy, is he not?"

It feels like my whole face is on fire. I swallow.

"*Is he not*?" Cristian repeats.

"Yes!"

"Then what's the problem, Greg?" He glares at me. "*Ignore* them both. I'm here with you, aren't I? You got what you wanted. So can you please cut this shit out?"

CHAPTER 26

"Hi, mister," Elijah says when I meet him at Grand Army Plaza the next day. It's Saturday. Our day. He looks more bleary-eyed and disheveled than usual. Cristian and I got home from Kate's birthday party before 1 a.m. For Elijah, it looks like, the night kept going well after that. I try not to think about what that entailed.

"Someone had fun last night," I say, because I do have to acknowledge his outing with Russell to the awards ceremony. It would be weird for me not to, especially since Elijah already knows I look at his Instagram stories.

Smiling shyly, he slides his hands into the pockets of his stylish shorts. "Yeah."

"So…" I begin, taking a long breath. "I want to apologize."

A plea forms on Elijah's face. "No, Greg, don't, please." He closes the distance between us. "You have nothing to apologize for." He wraps his arms around my waist and presses his forehead into the nook of my neck.

"No, no, I do," I say. "I was being ridiculous."

"You weren't, though."

"I shouldn't have acted the way I acted. I get like that sometimes. I overthink things and get too worked up. And, yes, maybe I got a little jealous, too. I'm sorry. It was totally unfair. Obviously, you're free to see whomever you want to see."

And, that, right there, as much as it pains me, is the reality and the truth. Elijah is his own man, and, like Cristian said, I need to cut this shit out. My opinion of Russell hasn't changed, but I do need to change my approach. Or rather, forget about an approach altogether.

Forget about Russell.

The guy is a psycho. I have no doubt about that. But I can now see how he's turning *me* into one, too. I need to ignore the fucker entirely, stop feeding him my anger and my reactions because that's exactly what he wants. All that's done is sour my relationships with Cristian and Elijah. I'm done fighting with my husband. I'm going to be patient. At the latest, Russell will be out of my life in a little over a month when the baby comes and Cristian will have to drop his ass, no questions asked.

Besides, I'm kind of out of options. Short of beating the shit out of the creep and potentially going to jail, what else can I do? I need to be the bigger man. I'm about to be a father. I should set a good, sensible example.

Of course, forgetting about Russell won't be as easy as I'd like. Even before we arrive at the Citi Bikes that will take us from Park Slope down to Sunset Park, Elijah brings up the awards ceremony again.

"Sophie was so nice," he says.

"Sophie?"

"The actress!"

"Ah, right…"

Animated, Elijah keeps on talking. Whenever the road gets devoid of cars, he rides his bike up beside mine and babbles on and on about all the celebrities he saw, what those celebrities said in their speeches, what they ate at their fancy tables. And what can I do but smile and listen? Elijah's a bright-eyed, twenty-two-year-old in the big city. He spent his Friday night mingling with famous people. Anyone would want to discuss that.

Objectively, I know this. And yet, the entire time he speaks, jealousy gnaws at my insides and my hate for Russell swells. Knowing that I could never take Elijah to something that cool and sophisticated doesn't help. Neither do the facts that Russell is wealthier than I am, and that his career and connections are more exciting.

But I'm not letting any of that intimidate me.

"Pee break," I yell and swerve from the street into the sprawling park.

"The toilets are that way!" Elijah yells behind me.

"I know," I call back, but keep going anyway.

Even though it's a cloudy day, Prospect Park is swarming with Brooklynites pushing strollers and being dragged by French bulldogs on leashes. Our bikes dodge joggers in yoga pants and teenagers hiding vodka bottles in brown paper bags.

As we go deeper, though, the number of people dwindles. I follow the winding paths until I find a narrow dirt one obstructed by leaves and branches. Entering it, I stand up to pedal and follow it all the way up to the top of a small hill.

Once there, I jump off and lean my bike against a tree. By the time Elijah catches up and lowers his to the ground, I already have my dick in my hand and I'm aiming a stream of piss at a small bush. Elijah lines up next to me and pulls out his own. We look at each other and smile.

When I finish, I step back to give Elijah his space. But the moment he's done shaking and turns around, I pounce. "Those are coming down anyway," I say into his mouth, my fingers fumbling with his shorts.

Startled only for a second, Elijah melts into my kiss. But when I yank his boxer-briefs down to his knees, he tenses up again. "Someone will see," he whispers.

"So?" I say with a smirk.

Elijah relaxes. A naughty grin takes shape on his lips as well. His gaze boring into mine, he slowly lowers himself to his knees.

Grabbing the base of my dick, I slap it against his face. A fire builds in Elijah's eyes, a silent defiance. It turns me on even more.

I slap him again. Then I put my hand on the back of his head and shove my cock deep into his throat. He gags and tears up, but he doesn't seem to mind.

When I'm close, I let him know. "Ready?" I moan.

He grunts in confirmation.

I shoot on his tongue. Seconds later, he speckles the ground.

As we're both zipping up, I lean in to kiss him. The tangy taste of my own cum spreads over my tongue. "That was so hot," Elijah says.

For the rest of the day, there's a big grin on my face. Sure, Russell may be ahead of me in a lot of other areas, but I can still compete with him in this one.

CHAPTER 27

"Excited about the baby shower?" Kate asks through her veggie panini at Bryant Park on an especially scorching August day.

"Yes! Thank you again for organizing everything."

"Hon," she says. "You know I love doing that type of shit."

"You're the best." Beaming at her, I unwrap my tuna melt sandwich from it's aluminum casing. The sun is so powerful today only a handful of people sit out on the open grass. Kate and I got super lucky with a table in the shade.

"What's going on with Russell?" she asks. "You haven't said anything about him in a while."

"Don't know and don't care," I reply.

"Is he still seeing Cristian?"

"I think so."

"And Elijah?"

"Probably."

"And it doesn't bother you anymore?"

"Honestly," I say with a sigh, "not really. I spend plenty of time with Cristian. Whenever Cristian has plans, I hang out with Elijah. I stopped bringing Russell up altogether and they

193

don't either. Russell just sort of stopped mattering."

"Has he, like, harassed you again or done anything else?" Kate asks.

"Nope."

"Okay, yeah," she says. "He's probably just one of those creepy assholes who thrive on attention. Once you stop giving it to them, they fuck off."

"Exactly," I say. "Cristian will have to stop seeing him soon. I'll have to stop seeing Elijah—but on *my* time, not on Russell's. After that, well, Elijah is an adult. He can make his own decisions. Either way, for me, it's going to be bye-bye Russell forever. I don't know why I let that piece of shit get to me like that in the first place."

Kate raises her water bottle and waits for me to do the same. "That's the spirit."

I pick up mine and bump it with hers.

After a sigh, I say, "I still have to tell Elijah about my deadline."

She sits up. "Excuse me? You *still* haven't?"

I feel a sting of shame. With everything that's been going on, I still haven't brought it up. But I'd also be lying if I said there wasn't a selfish part of me that kept putting it off out of fear of potentially alienating him. Causing him to leave my life before I was ready. "No," I reply. "Although he might've heard about it already from Russell."

"You have to tell him yourself, Greg. *Stat.*"

"I know," I say, as an idea on how I can go about that enters my mind. "I will. I'll do it this weekend."

For Friday night through Sunday, I rent a car and a little

creek-side cottage upstate in the Catskill Mountains. The plan is to enjoy the first night and tell Elijah about our imminent break-up on the second.

Considering it'll just be the two of us in a small cottage in the middle of nowhere, this might not be the best course of action. I like to think that he'll be cool with it, supportive even, but the truth is, I have no idea how the kid will react.

Technically, I could just tell Elijah over a drink at a dive bar. No need for trips and unnecessary expenses. But I want to convey to him that he's special to me. That the time we spent together these past few months meant something. And, of course, that I hope to still keep seeing him for the next few weeks, until the very end.

Cristian is even more encouraging than usual. He knows our deadline is looming and wants me to wrap things up with Elijah however I need to. And as much as I may not want to, and as hard as it may be, I do need to.

Overall, I think the trip is a good idea. Knowing that, for almost three days straight, Elijah will be with me, having sex with only me and not with Russell, feels kind of good, too.

Friday afternoon, when I pick him up in the rented Hyundai, he's wearing brown hiking boots and there's a chic safari hat on his head. He looks absolutely edible. He throws his engorged backpack into the backseat and climbs in to give me a kiss.

"You know it's only two nights, right?" I say teasingly as I eye the backpack.

"Yes, I'm aware," he says, beaming. He yanks off the hat and fixes his hair. "But it's our first trip together. I'm excited."

I just smile, gulp, and turn my attention to the road.

The drive is about two and a half hours. Passing through

the Bronx I discover that Elijah is a fan of Nina Simone and that he has a really mellow singing voice. An hour later, when the towering housing projects have been replaced by round, deliciously green mountains, I learn that the CIA employs a lot of Mormons.

"Why?" I ask.

"Apparently," he says, "my people are valued for being incorruptible."

Before we reach our destination, we make a stop at a little, rustic grocery store to stock up for the weekend. I suggest we stick to the basics—meats and vegetables we can throw on the grill—so we have more time to just lounge around. Elijah happily agrees.

Upstate, the air is a few notches cooler in comparison to the dense August heat of Brooklyn. The cold, pebble-bottomed creek is just down the hill behind our cottage, so as soon as our food is in the fridge, we go down for a dip. After we fuck and eat dinner, we do a repeat dip, this time, sans any swimwear. As Elijah runs back up the hill to the house, I laugh at the pale cheeks of his perky ass, still visible in the encroaching darkness.

The next morning, we sleep in. After we grab some egg sandwiches in the Hunter town center, Elijah puts on his safari hat, and we drive over to a scenic waterfall, where we take a ton of pics that end up on Elijah's Instagram. I really hope Russell sees them.

The rest of the day we spend eating, fucking, and lounging by the creek. We get a surprise visitor in the form of a wild turkey, and Elijah tells me that one of his dreams is to one day live in Europe, if only for a while. "Like you did, mister."

But then the sun hides behind the mountains and it's dark

and chilly and we're wearing flannel shirts in front of our make-shift campfire, and we're making s'mores, and the time for *me* to tell Elijah something finally arrives.

"Hey, cute stuff?" I say.

He glances up from the marshmallow pierced on his stick. The light from the flames dances across his smile. "What?"

I swallow. "So Cristian and I have been talking lately…" I choose to word it this way—like this is a thing that came about recently—because it's easier and I don't want him to think of me as a liar.

"Yeah…"

"And I think we're going to close the marriage again when the baby comes."

Elijah's smile vanishes. But his illuminated eyes remain fixed on me. The crackle of the fire is the only sound. The longer this lasts, the tighter my chest gets. "I'm sorry," I go on, focusing on retrieving my stick because I can't maintain eye contact.

When I look at Elijah again, I see a knot between his eyebrows and a strain in his jaw. "So what?" he asks. "I have to stop seeing you?"

"I'm sorry…"

"But I *love* you."

I flinch. Something within me expands. I almost say it back. A part of me really wants to—I care about this kid so much, I want to lessen his pain.

But I don't.

"We still have a month," I tell him.

He doesn't reply. He keeps staring at me, his lips pinched, his nostrils flaring. The marshmallow he was roasting has completely melted off.

"You're an asshole," he finally says.

My chest is so tight by now it hurts. I want to tell him, both for his benefit as well as my own, that there will likely come a time when Cristian and I will open up again. But I can't bring myself to do it. It'll only make this more complicated. "Elijah…"

"Russell was right about you."

I cringe at the name. It's dirty. Intrusive. It doesn't belong in this moment.

"He told me that you didn't actually care about me," he continues. "That you were only after sex, that you'd do anything to get some dick."

Hatred for Russell quickens my pulse, even though I'm not at all surprised. "That's not true and you know it."

"Oh yeah? Why do I have an expiration date then?"

Ashamed, I drop my gaze to the fire.

That night, Elijah sleeps with his back to me. I barely sleep at all. I'm angry with myself. For not having told him sooner, for hurting him, for letting my relationship with him progress this far in the first place. I'm angry about the fact that Russell will get to keep seeing him, even though he doesn't deserve to, and I won't.

I'm angry for many reasons. But I'm also sad.

On the way back to the city the next day, Elijah doesn't sing.

CHAPTER 28

The baby shower is mostly a blur. Cristian and I flank Amelia and her massive, round belly on Kate's sofa. I smile politely and make a convincing spectacle of unwrapping all the gifts, but, the truth is, I'm still bummed out over Elijah.

I haven't heard from the kid in days. I haven't reached out to him either.

"Oh, wow," I exaggerate, "it's a…" I have to read the box because I have no idea what the gift I'm holding actually is. "It's a healing ointment set!" I follow Cristian's gaze to where Jared, Cristian's friend from the studio, is hovering with his wife. "Thank you so much," Cristian and I singsong in by-now practiced unison. Amelia just nods. Her excitement is just not the same when there are gifts involved and they're not for her.

"What's on your mind?" Cristian asks me at home afterwards, while we're unloading our haul of presents. "You're so quiet."

"Nothing, mi amor," I say, giving him a peck. "I'm just a little tired. I think I'll go in the bedroom and read for a bit. Maybe take a nap."

An hour or so later, I get thirsty, so I put the parenting book I'm barely reading aside on the bed, and head over to the kitchen. In the living room, I try to talk to Cristian but he's so absorbed in what's playing on TV—some kind of mystery with a spunky female protagonist—he barley listens. I fill up a glass with water and let him be.

On the way back to the bedroom, I make a stop in our daughter's room. I see the crib squeezed into one corner, the shelves stocked with toys squeezed into another. We have towers of diaper packs in different sizes to last us for months. I smile.

When I'm leaving the room, a familiar voice reaches my ears. At first, I think I must be imagining it, but as I back up into the living room to make sure, I hear it again.

"Can you rewind that real quick?" I ask, my heart thundering.

Cristian's eyes are still glued to the TV. "What?"

"Can you—" But then I stop talking. Because there's no need for Cristian to rewind anything. Because there, on screen, clad in a police uniform and talking to the spunky female detective, is Elijah.

My knees buckle. "What are you watching?" I ask.

"Oh," Cristian says, finally ripping his gaze away from the screen. "It's a Netflix show." He looks slightly uncomfortable, maybe even guilty. "One of Russell's," he continues to explain, even though he doesn't need to. By now, I've figured it out for myself. "I promised him I'd watch it." Cristian's voice is timid. "They're filming the new season now. Some of it is set in Brazil. It's pretty interesting, I guess."

Brazil.

Through the lump in my throat, I say, "That was Elijah."

"What?"

"One of the cops earlier. That was Elijah."

Cristian's brow wrinkles. "Really?" He sits up. "Should I rewind it?"

"No need."

"I thought you said he worked for some meal delivery company?"

"Yeah," I say. "That's what he told me."

For a few beats, we're silent. Cristian appears concerned but unsure. "That explains why Russell and Elijah know each other, I guess," he says.

I draw a shaky breath. "I'm going out for a bit."

The betrayal I feel as I leave the apartment is a hyena feasting on my most delicate organs. No matter how you look at it, Elijah knew Russell before he knew me. A simple Internet search tells me that the Netflix show has been out for months. I only know Elijah for three. He lied to me. I have an idea as to why, but I don't want it to be true. Before I allow myself to believe it, I need to hear it from his mouth.

I need to see you, I text. *It's important.*

A minute later, Elijah replies with: *Our bar in twenty minutes?*

The whole way, in the Uber, I'm shaking. I feel like such an idiot. Of course Elijah was too good to be true. Of course he doesn't actually love me. All of his kind words. All of his touches, smiles, tears. Lies. All of it *fucking lies*.

When he walks up to the table I'm waiting at with my vodka, there's a cautious smile on his face. There's hesitance in it and sadness and hope. He's a good actor.

201

I don't smile back. "I saw your work," I say as soon as he sits down across from me. His smile, already on the way out, vanishes completely. "You play a convincing police officer." I pause. "And lover. Obviously."

He leans back in his chair, observing me. And in that moment, right before my eyes, he transforms into a complete stranger. He stops being the curious, bright-eyed all-American boy I have come to know these past few months. He still looks young to me—I doubt he lied about his age—but he no longer looks innocent.

"What," he says. "It's not like you didn't withhold information from me either. You said nothing about your deadline until the Catskills trip. Not to mention everything you failed to tell Russell—about the deadline, the baby. Being married, even."

"Is he paying you?" I ask, my voice cracking.

Elijah snorts. "Of course not."

"So what is it?"

"What's the problem, though?" he presses. "We had fun. We had tons of great sex. We each got what we wanted from each other. So we held a few things back about ourselves. So what? It's not like we were going to be together forever."

"Cut the crap, Elijah," I snap, but there's a hitch to my voice. My heart is thrumming in my ears. "Can you just tell me truth? Please?"

His expression softens. "Look, Greg," he says. "You're a good guy. I genuinely like you." A pause. "But, the truth is, it's *Russell* I love."

Nothing about this should surprise me. With how conniving, how manipulative, how *charming* Russell can be, it's no wonder he'd have a young actor like Elijah wrapped around his finger. But the words are still a knife plunged into my gut. "So why would you do this?" I ask. "Why not just be with him? Why fuck with me?"

Elijah looks at me like he doesn't quite understand.

"Because he asked me to," he replies.

CHAPTER 29

When I get home, I find Cristian on the sofa with his glasses on and his lit-up phone in his hands. "So what happened?" he asks. "What did Elijah say?"

"Nothing," I answer, coldly, as I kick off my shoes. "It doesn't matter."

"I texted Russell," he continues, indicating his phone. "He said he doesn't know what Elijah told you but he's known Elijah for about two years."

"It doesn't *matter*," I repeat. "I don't *care* anymore." I catch Cristian's gaze and hold it. "I don't want to hear about Russell ever again. *Ever*. Got it?"

Cristian's shoulders droop. Frowning, he looks back down at his screen, and replies with a soft: "Got it."

In silence, I wash my hands at the kitchen sink, grab a cold beer from the fridge, and shut myself in the bedroom where I play an Almodóvar film on my laptop.

I could tell Cristian all about what Elijah told me. But what's the point? What would that accomplish besides lead to another fight and an unnecessary admittance of just how much I cared for the kid, how much what I learned today hurt me?

Russell won. He got what he wanted. He succeeded in making me look like a fool. In punishing me. Or whatever the fuck it was he was trying to do. It's over. I'm done.

Never again will Russell be the cause of an argument between my husband and me. Never again will he make my teeth grit with fury and my heart pound with frustration. Never again will I give him that power. Russell and Elijah? They no longer exist to me. As far as I'm concerned, they never did. I don't even want to think about them. I just want to put all of this *shit*—these past few months from hell—behind me.

I have to. Or else I'll go crazy.

That Sunday, Cristian and I have dinner plans with Amelia.

In the last two weeks since I last saw her, it seems like her belly has doubled in size. I didn't think it was possible. The woman looks enormous and clunky and beautiful.

As is his routine, when Cristian sees her in front of the Italian restaurant, he gives her a huge hug and then drops to his knees to do the same thing to her protruding midriff.

Once he's done, I surprise everyone by taking his place. It's not like I've never touched Amelia's belly before. I have. But I usually just lower myself to my haunches and maintain a respectable distance, making contact only with my palms. This time, however, my knees plop to the sidewalk and my forehead connects to the bulging front of Amelia's maternity dress. I feel her stiffen but she lets me do this.

"Hi, baby," I say. "I love you."

When I stand back up, both Amelia and Cristian are quiet,

looking stunned, as if they'd just witnessed me levitate.

"What?" I ask.

"Nothing," Amelia says. "Shall we? I'm starving."

Our plates of creamy mushroom fettuccine laid out in front of us, we each make our case for our favorite baby names. I've always liked the name Joanne, but I'm quickly overruled. Apparently, it's too old school and too basic.

As the evening goes on, a calming tide settles over me. This is what matters, I think. This is the only place my mind should have been these past few months. I wish I had a redo. I wish I'd never met Russell, never met Elijah. I wish my husband and I closed up as soon as Amelia got pregnant. But it's okay, I tell myself. It's still not too late for me to realize and appreciate that I'm one lucky motherfucker.

I reach under the table to squeeze Cristian's hand. He turns to me and smiles. Everything's perfect until Amelia says:

"Oh! Russell texted me this morning."

I jerk my hand away from Cristian's. "What did you just say?" I ask.

Amelia looks at me like I insulted her. "Russell. The TV producer?"

Suddenly, I'm sweating all over. Cristian's avoiding my gaze.

"Anyway," Amelia goes on, "He wanted to introduce me to his good friend Gwen, who's also pregnant. So, I was, like, yeah, sure. He gave me her number and I FaceTimed with her for a bit. Turns out we have *so much* in common. She's also giving birth to a little girl and her due date is only two months after mine. And listen to this: she goes to the same doctor! Dr. Sanders didn't inseminate her, obviously, her husband did that himself—or so she claims—but still. And the best part?" Amelia pauses for dramatic effect. "She has a house on St. Bart's and she's flying out there soon and wants me to come along so I can recover from the labor and talk to her about it."

The whole time she's babbling, I'm observing Cristian. It almost seems like he's shrinking in size. "How does Amelia know Russell?" I ask, interrupting her.

"Oh," Amelia answers on his behalf. "We hang out *all the time.*"

"Amelia," Cristian chides.

"Cristian," I say. "*What* is she talking about?"

"Twice," he says. "She hung out with him twice."

"Last time," Amelia says, eagerly, "we went to karaoke in Koreatown."

Having to control my breathing is turning into a chore. "You introduced Russell to *Amelia*?" I ask. "The mother of our child?"

Once again, Cristian drops his gaze to his pasta.

"What's the problem?" Amelia asks, but there's a glint in her eye that suggests she knows exactly what the problem is. What bringing up Russell would do.

"Nothing," I say, re-focusing on my plate, even though inside, my emotions are holding a riot. I'm furious at Cristian for crossing a major line. At Russell for always finding a way to drill himself into my life—especially now, after I thought I'd finally managed to purge him from it. "Let's just finish our dinner."

In the taxi, on the way home, however, as soon as the doors shut, I explode.

"What the *fuck*, Cristian?" I say. "Why would you do that? You know how I feel about Russell and all the shit he did to me and you introduce him to fucking *Amelia*?"

"It wasn't intentional," he replies. "I was with her and he was nearby."

"So you *unintentionally* asked him to come join you?"

Cristian goes quiet. I watch the lights from outside storefronts and billboards bounce across his contemplative face.

"You know she's going to stay in touch with him," I continue, my body trembling. "Russell was supposed to be out of our lives in a couple of weeks and now she's getting chummy with his social circle? What were you thinking?"

Cristian's eyes are locked on the back of our driver's head.

"I'm sorry," he says.

"You should be." Facing the window on my side, I say, "I guess we don't have to get Amelia that tropical getaway we were planning anymore, since Russell is hooking her up with a much better one we could never afford." Feeling too hot all of a sudden, I press the button and a window slides down, letting in the evening breeze. "Why are you even still hanging out with him?" I continue. "The baby's almost here."

"Did you already stop hanging out with your guys?" Cristian asks.

"Yes," I say. "Actually, I did."

There's a glint of surprise in Cristian's voice. "Why?"

"What do you mean *why*? Because we agreed to stop seeing other people when the baby is born and the baby is almost here. Why else?"

For a few beats, Cristian is silent again.

"Maybe that wasn't such a good idea," he says.

I whip my face his way. "What wasn't?"

"Maybe we shouldn't close back up."

Panic accelerates my heart. Cristian? Suggesting we keep

the relationship open? I never thought I'd see the day. "You can't be serious," I say. "I *want* us to close up. I thought that's what you wanted, too. And now, here I am, completely ready and willing to give that to you, and you're singing an entirely different tune?"

"It's a big change," he continues. "Instead of helping, closing up the marriage again at this stage might only cause unnecessary tension between us, lead to unnecessary stress. In the end, that tension might even affect the baby."

Something in me fractures.

"Are you *in love* with him?" I ask, my voice catching.

He sighs. "With whom?"

"You know damn well with whom."

Rather than answer, Cristian looks me in the eyes. His face is a shadowed mask of sadness. "Greg," he says, softly. "Why are you doing this? I thought you'd be happy. I know how important sex and sexual expression are to you."

"Answer me," I press. Maybe I'm being a dick, maybe this is only my insecurity talking, but I need to make sure I still have a grip on Cristian. If Russell's gotten to him too, I don't know what I'll do. "Are you in love with Russell?"

Cristian averts his gaze, bites his bottom lip. He's shaking his head, but when his eyes lock with mine again, I wake up to just how far apart we've grown lately. It's almost like he's suddenly wearing a lock I don't know the combination to anymore.

"No, Greg," he says, quietly. "I'm not in love with Russell."

He sounds sincere. I want to believe him.

But Russell is a vicious animal.

And I believed Elijah, too.

CHAPTER 30

Directly across the street from the Williamsburg studio where Cristian works, there's a plain, unmarked warehouse with a wide garage door and a regular-sized door beside it. Because the ground here slopes downward, towards the East River, the regular-sized door has a step, and, because I've never seen that door open, I always sit on that step while I wait for Cristian to finish up work and come out.

Not today. Today, I'm at the other end of the block, just around the corner of a graffiti-adorned brick building, watching the studio from afar.

Cristian doesn't know I'm here. He thinks I'm out on a date but I only told him I have one tonight because I know that he does. And even though I don't have any evidence that it's with Russell, I'm willing to cut my dick off that it is.

I need to see them together. Find out for myself just how far their relationship has progressed. How much of a threat it is to my relationship with Cristian.

When Russell started seeing my husband, I was pissed off at

Russell and worried about Cristian's safety. But that's it. The idea that Russell could be an actual threat to what Cristian and I have cultivated together over so many years, something I believed to be untouchable, invincible, hadn't even occurred to me.

But I was a fool. Russell is poison. He's a dangerous parasite, capable of inflicting incredible amounts of damage. I need to find out the extent of it.

After my husband went to sleep last night, I did something taboo. For the first time in our relationship, I took his phone into the bathroom and attempted to unlock it without his knowledge. I tried different combinations—important dates, birthdays, variations that included Cristian's favorite number: four—but none of it worked.

Today, I left the office two hours early, telling my boss I had another doctor's appointment of Amelia's I needed to be present for. Before coming to Williamsburg, I made a stop at our apartment and searched the place, but I'm not sure what I was even looking for. What incriminating evidence was I hoping to find? A love letter? Hidden videos of Cristian and Russell's love-making?

When 6 p.m. rolls around, the door to Cristian's studio opens, spitting out five of his coworkers, some of whom I recognize. Together, they head in the opposite direction of where I am, like I expect them to. I purposefully chose the end of the block that's farther away from the train.

A couple of minutes later, the studio door swings open again. Out of it juts the front wheel of a bike, followed by Jared, whom I'd most recently seen at our baby shower. Swiftly, he jumps on the bike and starts charging in my direction. Panicking, I pull down my baseball cap and face the wall. As he whizzes by behind me, I'm down near the ground, pretending to tie my shoe. He doesn't see me.

By 6:30, I start to grow impatient, even though it's taken Cristian this long to come out in the past. When the clock hits 7:30 p.m., however—by which time I've witnessed more than ten people leave the studio and more than ten Williamsburg couples stroll by carrying grocery bags from Whole Foods—my impatience turns to confusion. Cristian never works this late. Is it possible that he's not even *at* work today? That he's been canoodling with Russell since morning? The thought makes me sick to my stomach.

A hip, shorthaired Asian woman makes an exit next. As she shuts the studio door behind her, her gaze is fixed on her phone. I've never seen her before and I don't recall Cristian ever talking about anyone who fits her description, but when I see that she's coming my way, I decide to speak to her anyway.

"Hi," I say from my hiding place. Understandably, she startles. "Sorry!" I quickly add when I see her freeze up. "I'm Cristian's partner, Greg. Sorry to bug you. You don't happen to know if he's still in there, do you?"

She relaxes. "Yeah, he's still in there with Levi."

"Thank you," I say. "Sorry if I scared you."

"No worries," she replies and returns to her phone.

The Williamsburg sky turns pink, then purple, then finally a dark, dark blue before all sunlight disappears altogether. It's nearing 9 p.m., Cristian is still inside, and I'm beyond pissed. What could he possibly be doing?

The girl said he was in there with Levi, a Dutch guy I've met once at an exhibition opening party. From what I remember, Levi works on the administrative side of things, doing marketing and PR and the like, so it makes sense that he'd be working later than the production team. Is Cristian helping him with that? But he never does.

It's while I'm thinking this that, finally, my husband emerges. I feel a rush of exhilaration. His eyes are on his phone but I slip behind the brick wall of the corner anyway, just in case. After a few seconds, I peek around and see his backside, illuminated by an orange streetlamp, as he retreats in the direction of the train station. I'm about to follow him when my phone pings with a new text.

My heart speeds up. It's from Cristian.

I'm done with dinner, it says, *heading home now*.

In a flash, betrayal and confusion constrict my throat. Cristian is lying. He didn't go to dinner. He never had a date with Russell. He's right there. What is happening?

Once Cristian disappears from view, I shuffle through the quiet street in his path, racking my brain about what all of this could mean. But when I'm passing the door to the studio, something makes me stop. Facing it, I raise a finger to the intercom installed into the wall beside it.

"Yes?" I hear when Levi answers.

"Hey, Levi," I say, "It's Greg. Cristian's partner. Cristian forgot something."

"Oh," he replies, "okay. Hold on."

A minute later, the door swings open. "Hey," Levi says, backlit by a small ceiling lamp in the studio's vestibule. The best word to describe the late twenty-something-year-old is "shaggy". Levi's dirty blond curls and slightly darker beard are in total disarray, but the effect is closer to charming than repulsive. From time to time, Cristian will complain to me about how impatient the man can be, but, overall, they're on good terms. "What's up?" Levi asks, looking around behind me. "Where's Cristian?"

"He, um, had to run home," I answer. "Something urgent." I clear my throat. "He asked me to get something from his locker, said you'd still be here."

Levi frowns. "I hope everything's okay," he says. His pronunciation of the "th" in "everything" sounds more like an "s", betraying his Dutch upbringing.

"It is!" I say. "Everything's fine. Thank you. Sorry to bug you."

"No worries. I'm about to leave shortly, too. Come on in."

Since it's not a customer-facing operation and since the Dutch artist Cristian works for tends to be secretive about his projects, outsiders are rarely allowed inside the studio. Work parties and exhibitions always happen off its grounds, so there's no real reason for anyone who doesn't work there to go inside. But sometimes, after hours, while the team he leads is still cleaning up, Cristian will invite me in to wait for him, especially during wintertime when it's freezing outside.

"The locker room is just over there." Levi says, "You know where, right?"

"I do, thanks," I say. "Was Cristian helping you with something today?"

"No, no, he's still working on his own thing."

"Gotcha," I reply, even though I have no idea what Levi's talking about. The way he says that, however, makes me feel like I should. Pressure builds in my chest. What else don't I know about Cristian? What else is he hiding from me?

"I'll be at my desk upstairs," Levi says. "Holler on your way out."

"I will," I say. "Thank you."

The men's locker room has just enough space to fit maybe three or four people at a time. I open the metal cabinet bearing Cristian's name. I have no idea what I'm looking for, but whatever it is, I don't find it. Besides a pair of slippers, two coveralls hanging from hangers, and various patriotic pictures of Picasso, Julio Iglesias, and Penélope Cruz taped to the inside walls, there's nothing else in it.

I check all the paint-stained coverall pockets, only to discover they're empty, and close the locker. But I don't leave just yet. I sneak past the vestibule and the stairs that lead to the second floor where Levi is and venture deeper into the studio.

Most of the lights are off, but it's still easy to make out the spacious, interconnected rooms, even if they're enveloped in shadow. I walk past shelves of paint jars and stacks of canvas rolls and into the studio's main area. It's a giant space that reaches all the way to the roof of the two-story building and which could comfortably fit a Mack truck. This is where most of the production work takes place. In the middle, the wall-sized painting Cristian's team is currently working on lies flat on the floor. It's covered with sheets of protective paper for the night so I'm unable to see what it portrays.

There's little else in there of interest. I walk through and out the other end, which connects to yet another, smaller space filled with a few desks and computer monitors. I find Cristian's—I spot a photo of us on the beach in Greece—but, as expected, it's password-protected. I'm mostly relieved. I've already overstayed my welcome.

With the full intention of leaving, I pass through the final space in the building, a large room full of sinks and boxes. But there's also a closed door there. Cursing under my breath—because the closed door probably just leads to another storage space and what the hell am I even doing—I beeline for it.

But it's not a storage space. The room the door opens into is almost entirely empty. All it contains is a chair and an easel holding up a painting. The painting is about the size of a window and it's facing away from the entrance. Slowly, I make my way toward it. It's also covered in protective paper, but something tells me to lift it.

And so I do. With my fingers, I clasp the bottom edge of the airy material and flip it over until the painting is fully visible.

At first, for what feels like minutes, my throat and lungs constrict to such a degree, I can't breathe. But then, in a torrent of tiny gasps, air starts passing through me again.

Russell is completely naked. I can see all the hairs on his jaw, on his chest, on his abs and calves. I recognize his prominent clavicle bone and the mole on his thigh. The leftward curve of his cock and his low-hanging balls.

Cross-armed, he's leaning back against the railing of a balcony. The cityscape behind him—which I'd only seen from that balcony in the evening—is as familiar to me as the piercing, blue stare Russell is giving the viewer.

On the easel, in the bottom right corner, sits a Polaroid photo. The painting is its almost exact, magnified replica, except it somehow manages to surpass the photo in both realism and intimacy. But that's Cristian's talent for you.

Tears pool in my eyes.

The painting is at an advanced stage. And it's magnificent. Cristian must've spent weeks working on it. Pouring into it his entire heart.

CHAPTER 31

The next evening, Cristian does meet up with Russell. I know this not because he tells me, but because I'm there to witness it happen in person, albeit from afar.

Flickers of candlelight dance across Russell's handsome, bearded face. He lifts the glass containing his amber-colored whiskey up to the grin on his lips. After he takes a sip, the grin erupts into a big, masculine laugh—one of those bold, limitless ones only a man with looks, money, and power can unleash.

The shirt he's wearing tonight is a shade of pink, a detour from the usual crispy white he's trademarked. On brand, however, its top two buttons are undone, exposing his chest hair. Under the table, his muscular thighs fill out his neat pants to a T.

A hand lands on one of those thighs. It only stays there for a brief moment, but that doesn't matter. What matters is that my husband places it there in the first place.

In my dark corner, on the other side of the bar from where Cristian and Russell are huddled over a small table, I try to contain a violent surge of panic. It lingers there, just below the surface, but then retreats.

Elijah's sole purpose was to distract. I know that now. The boy wasn't supposed to make me fall in love with him, or to hurt me, or even make me look like an idiot. He was simply there to keep my attention away from…*this*.

The only other time I've seen Cristian and Russell together was that first time, when I walked in on them in our apartment. Even though Cristian was completely naked then, and even though the two of them had clearly just wrapped up a sexual encounter, what I witnessed at the time was nowhere near the level of intimacy on display here. Watching them now, I feel completely unnecessary. Like a hindrance even, an inflamed appendix. If Cristian just cut me out, he'd be so much better off.

Downing the rest of my vodka, I lower the bill of my baseball cap and get up. I can't bear to see my husband look at that snake like that any longer.

Outside, on the street, I take out my phone and open Grindr. I realize it's been weeks since I last did. Between Elijah and preparing for the baby I just didn't have the time. There's a familiar comfort in being back on. Immediately, Grindr transports me to another, less turbulent world.

Russell brought Cristian to a hip, new bar in Harlem. I'm rarely in these parts so most of the profiles I see are new to me and vice versa. With trembling fingers, I scroll through the men on my screen. Or, rather, through their various body parts—chests, arms, backs, thighs. Within minutes I attract over ten messages.

Looking? I get from a guy who reminds me of a young Mario Lopez—if young Mario Lopez had a buzz cut and a five o'clock shadow.

Yeah, I reply. *Hosting?*

Yeah.

Hit with adrenaline, I send more photos, including my nudes with face, which I don't normally do, but tonight I don't give a fuck. I ask for him to return the favor. He does and five minutes later I'm halfway to his address.

What apartment? I ask when I arrive.

5B. Walk-up. Sorry.

On the fifth floor, my heart rate raised from the climb, I knock on his door.

Young Mario's definitely shorter than the 5′10″ he claims to be in his profile, but he's got a cute grin, and again, tonight, I don't give a fuck.

"Hey," he says.

"Hey," I respond, then look past him, inside his home.

He seems to pick up on my urgency because he steps aside. "Come on in," he says and leads me past one messy bedroom, then another—all the doors are wide open—before making a stop in the communal kitchen, which is only slightly less messy in comparison. "Would you like some water or something?"

"No thanks," I say. "You by yourself?"

"Yeah," he replies, no longer smiling. My mood must be contagious. "The roommates are both out."

"Cool." My eyes drift toward the nearest bedroom.

"So, um," he says. "Do you want to see my room?"

Once we're both naked, we kiss, but not for long. I turn him around and push at his back until he's on all fours on his bed. Spitting onto my hand, I lube up his ass. His body is stiff but he stays quiet, obedient. I don't worry about a condom, I don't ask him about PrEP. I just push myself inside.

Sweat dripping from my chest, I fuck him hard from behind until he disconnects himself and flips around. "Can you fuck me this way?" he asks, hoisting himself farther up on the bed. I shrug and crawl over to where he's waiting.

At one point, while we're fucking missionary, our chests pressed up together, he runs his fingers through my hair. His lips whisk along my face and neck. I let him do this but don't reciprocate. I just focus on the rhythm of my movements and the building pleasure. That's all I want from this boy. Mindless pleasure.

"Hey," he says.

At first, I ignore him. But when he sets both of his hands on each side of my face and says it for the third time, I have no choice but to look at him. His eyes are big with surprise but there's also a crease of worry on his forehead.

"You're crying," he tells me.

"No, I'm not," I say, but, realizing he's right, I completely lose my rhythm. I turn my face to the side. "I'm good," I say. "Sorry. Just give me a sec."

"What's wrong?" he asks.

It's the way he says it, with so much kindness and empathy. All at once, I become attuned to the immense sadness I'm carrying around. To the colossal fear I have of losing Cristian. All strength leaves my body. I stop thrusting and collapse on top of him.

He holds me while I sob into his neck. I don't know how long this lasts. Finally, I slide off him and flip onto my back, hiding my wet eyes in the crook of my arm. He doesn't talk right away. He lets me lie there in silence.

After a while, he asks: "Is it a guy?"

The memory of Cristian's hand on Russell's thigh enters my mind. I see them laughing, huddling close together. I grunt a, "Yeah," in reply.

"Were you happy with him?"

I feel silly discussing this with a stranger, this kid, who's probably ten years younger than me. And yet, I croak out, "Yeah. The happiest."

"He didn't die, did he?"

I force a snort. "No."

"Did you break up with him or did he break up with you?"

My throat tightens. "Neither."

"So you're still together?" he says. "That's good! It's not over yet."

"It pretty much is."

"How can you know that?"

"It's too late."

"Oh yeah? Can you honestly say that you did everything you can to keep him?"

The question takes me by surprise. "I think so…"

"Yeah," he says, "that means you *didn't*."

I hold my breath. My heart is pounding.

"Look," Young Mario goes on. "Mope around and be sad and all that shit *after* you're certain there's nothing left you can do. But first, *act*. Do whatever's necessary. It's like what my grandma used to say: If something means the world to you, you have to try everything in the world to keep it."

CHAPTER 32

At work, the next day, a hand touches down on my shoulder and I almost rocket out of my office chair. "Jesus," Kate says, withdrawing it like she burned it.

"Sorry," I say. "Is it lunchtime already?"

"Dude." She squints. "Your eyes are red as fuck. Are you high?"

I press my knuckles into my sockets. "No."

"Everything all right?"

"Yeah," I say, blinking rapidly. "Just really into this translation."

She glances at my computer screen. "Yeah, *so* fascinating." Her eyes drift back to me. She gives me a weak smile. "You look like shit."

"Thanks. I didn't get much sleep last night."

"Are you freaking out about the baby? Any day now."

I lift the corners of my lips. "You bet."

She doesn't look like she believes me. "Whatever it is, you're going to tell me all about it, yeah?" Strutting away, she points a finger at my chest. "See you in fifteen."

At lunch, we find a secluded table in the sitting area of a Madison Avenue deli. Our plates are stacked with food from the hot bar. Kate places her elbows around hers and, cradling her face in her hands, says, "Okay, I'm all ears."

Hearing the concern in her voice causes whatever costume of composure I've been wearing to crumble away completely.

"Greg," she says, her voice turning more serious. "What is it?"

Tears push at the back of my eyes. I shake my head.

"Greg?"

My chest feels so tight. I wasn't going to tell her anything. Especially since, after following Cristian and Russell last night, my mind has gone to some very, very dark places. I was going to think everything through some more, but I've done so much of that already, my brain is fried. Talking to my best friend can only help.

"I'm going to lose him, Kate."

Her frown deepens. "*Who*?"

"Cristian."

"What are you talking about?"

I want to go on, explain, but it's so hard to get the words out. At this point, I have to fight for my breath. "Russell…"

Kate places a hand on top of my tightly squeezed fist. "Hon, you're working yourself up. Here. Let's take a deep breath."

"I'm not."

"Take a deep breath," she orders. "Come on, do it with me. Ready? In…"

Taking her lead, I inhale a long shaky breath.

"…and out."

Together, we exhale. I glance in the direction of the three

Asian women sitting at a nearby table. They're all silent. And they're all looking at me.

"Good," Kate says. "Again. In…"

We repeat the process once, and then once more after that. It helps get my thoughts in line, but doesn't change the fact that I'm about to lose the love of my life.

"See?" Kate gives me a gentle smile. "Better?

"Russell's going to steal him from me."

Kate's lips pinch together. "What makes you say that?"

"If Cristian's not in love with him already, then he's well on his way."

"But *what* makes you say that?" she presses.

"I saw the way they are together."

"What do you mean? What exactly did you see?"

A tear slides down my cheek. I hold her gaze. "Do I have to explain it?"

Kate's expression softens. She nods in understanding. "And they were just doing this, acting like that in front of you?"

"No," I say. "I followed them."

For a beat, Kate just stares at me. Then, leaning forward, over her plate of food, she tightens her grip over my fist and says, "Think back to all the times in your life when you thought something bad was happening or *going* to happen and it never did. It always turned out okay in the end. Every time."

I had a feeling that if I said anything to Kate she'd eventually blame my anxiety. "This time it's different. I'm about to lose him, Kate. I'm *certain* of it."

"But Cristian loves you so much," she says. "It doesn't make sense. I'm sure there are things you don't know about. I'm sure this will work itself out."

"Just because he loves me doesn't mean he doesn't love Russell."

"Have you talked to him?" she challenges.

"I asked him directly if he had feelings for Russell and he denied it. I always believe everything he says, but this time, I'm positive he's lying. Or, at least, not telling me the whole truth. I can *feel* it." The lump in my throat swells. "He said he wants to stay open. He wants to keep seeing Russell even after the baby is born."

Her eyes turn into saucers. "Really?"

More tears spill out of me. "And he *painted* him, Kate. A beautiful portrait. Kept it a secret from me for weeks. I went to his studio and saw it."

Kate flinches. She's well aware that Cristian has never painted a portrait of me.

"I spent all night thinking about what I can do and there's nothing," I go on. "There's *nothing* I can do."

"We'll figure something out," she says, but her voice has lost conviction.

"And I already tried so many things," I continue. "First, I talked to Russell like an adult. Then I threatened him. When none of that worked, I took the higher road and tried ignoring him. And where did that get me?"

"Surely, Cristian would—"

"I thought about bribing him. But with the amount I'd be able to scrape together? He'd laugh in my face. Then I thought about blackmailing him somehow, but he knows all these people in high places. He has all these connections. I wouldn't even make a dent. I even thought about killing him, Kate. I swear, I actually considered it."

Kate's head tilts. "Please tell me you're joking."

"I need to act. Do *something*. Before it's too late. It might already be too late. Russell's evil. He intentionally came to steal what's mine."

"Are you fucking kidding me? *Kill* him?"

"He's untouchable otherwise. There's nothing else I can do."

"Right, so murder him then. That's smart. Oh! Maybe you can even do it on the day of your daughter's birth. Go to jail and leave Cristian to raise her by himself."

My voice shrinks. "I wouldn't get caught. If something means the world to you," I say, repeating the quote my hookup, Young Mario Lopez, shared with me last night in Harlem, "you have to try everything in the world to keep it."

"Stop!" she shouts. For a second, I think she might slap me, but she doesn't. Instead, she takes a deep breath and says, "There *is* something you can do. Go home to Cristian, Greg. Focus on the baby and what that baby means to you and your husband. Once the baby comes, Cristian will realize how much he loves you. I promise you. Russell won't matter. All of this will blow over. Once you're both holding your daughter in your arms, you'll realize that what *you and Cristian* have is untouchable."

"The baby's not going to change anything," I mutter. "Cristian wants to keep seeing him. I have to do something *now*."

"Leave work early today," Kate orders. "Go straight *home*. Get some sleep. When Cristian gets back from work, show him how much you love him. *Tell* him how much you love him. Don't even think about Russell. Don't give that bastard the time of day. The only people you should be thinking about are Cristian, the baby, and yourself."

I shake my head. "You don't understand..."

"Don't do anything drastic." She grabs my chin and holds it still. "Greg? Please. Do you hear me? Get some rest. We'll talk about this tomorrow. Things could be totally different by then. You'll feel better. Seriously, Greg. *Go home.*"

CHAPTER 33

I don't go home.

I do, however, leave work early. I take the M train downtown, just like I normally would, but before it can take me across the Williamsburg Bridge to Brooklyn, I get off it at Broadway-Lafayette, in SoHo. The sun hits my face when I step outside. It's a beautiful September day. I wish I were at the beach with Cristian.

I shuffle past tourists and shoppers until I'm seated at the same counter at the same Mediterranean restaurant I came to the last time I was in the area. I order the same vodka soda and I stare at the same building diagonally across the street.

Hours pass. I wouldn't notice otherwise, but the waitress comes around every half-hour or so to indicate my empty glass, yanking me out of my thoughts and reminding me to check the time. It's the afternoon—too late for lunch, too early for dinner—so the restaurant is basically empty. I don't order another vodka soda—I need to be sober for what I'm about to do—but I do ask the waitress for a coffee, just to get her off my back.

Kate doesn't understand the scope of the situation. Things

will blow over, she said. Give this some time, stop thinking about it, and you'll feel differently tomorrow. But she couldn't be more wrong. She's never met Russell. She doesn't know what he's capable of. How much of a bloodsucker he is. I can't just sit around and let him do more damage until that damage is irreversible. I can't just watch him steal my life.

A few minutes past five o'clock, across the street, at the very spot I've been staring at for hours, Russell materializes on the sidewalk.

As usual, he looks fantastic in his trademark attire of dress pants and shirt—two buttons undone, sleeves rolled up. Seeing him—with his air of offhand smugness, privilege, entitlement—only amplifies my hatred. I wish I'd swiped left on the bastard. All those months ago. I wish I never let him into my life.

He's walking, fast. I toss a few bills onto the counter next to my empty coffee cup and get up.

Because my eyes are glued to Russell, as I follow him, I bump shoulders with a tall teenage girl, then march straight into a Spanish-speaking couple a minute later. I apologize each time, even though I barely register any of them.

Once I realize that Russell's likely just walking home because it's so nice out and because his loft in Tribeca isn't far, I allow myself to relax a little. The farther downtown he goes, the thinner the crowds become. I maintain a reasonable distance. I'm not ready for him to see me. Not yet.

A good chunk of the time he spends with his eyes on his phone. When I catch sight of his trademark smirk, my throat closes up. Is he texting Cristian? On the other end, is Cristian smiling, too? Tiny gasps interrupt my breathing.

In Tribeca, I watch Russell enter a quiet block. He strolls

through it, all alone. For a moment, it's like watching a scene from a post-apocalyptic film. A lone man, crossing a desolate urban landscape. How easy it would be, I think. To follow him in, sneak up behind him. To snap his neck or slit his throat.

The mundane situation of Russell meeting his end in a deserted street while walking home from work would not only be efficient but also unexpected. Random. And random is impersonal. Random can be anytime, anywhere, any*one*.

When you develop a diseased limb, you cut it off, right? When there's a rat infestation, you call an exterminator. You get rid of things that pose a threat to your health and well-being. Russell Mailey is a threat to my health and well-being. My *family's* health and well-being. If he remains in the equation, I'll end up with nothing. Take him out of it and I'm the happiest man on earth.

Eventually, Russell reaches his street with its red and white brick buildings and their lofty windows and their steel fire escapes weaving across their facades. I've only been here in the evenings, after drinks or dinner, when the place was cloaked in a mix of darkness and artificial light. It looks odd now, feels too exposed in the bright afternoon sunlight. It's so much more alive as well, with the deliveryman and his truck and the old lady with a Beagle on a leash.

Russell stops in front of his building and steps inside.

I'm sweating profusely, crawling with nerves. I should wait a bit. Fifteen, maybe twenty minutes. I don't want it to look like I followed him home, even if that's exactly what I did. I think about running over to a deli to get a coffee, just to have something to do, but it's a risk. What if Russell leaves his home in the short time I'm away? I give up on the coffee and shuffle over to a small construction site, where I tuck myself behind the green fence enclosing a part of the sidewalk. From there, I watch the entrance to Russell's building and wait.

After eighteen excruciating minutes, I decide to go for it. I shoot out from my temporary hiding spot and march straight for Russell's address.

It's only when I see the middle-aged concierge's face and note his immediate reaction at seeing mine that I remember my previous encounter with the man. My mind's been so fixated on Russell himself, I've failed to consider all potential obstacles. The last time the concierge and I interacted was the night I'd learned that, in addition to seeing my Cristian, Russell was also seeing Elijah. I was drunk and violent and this presently scowling man escorted me out of the building.

"You're not welcome here," he says, standing up, both of his hands hidden behind the reception desk.

"I'm sorry about last time."

"Please leave."

I lift both arms, palms out. "I promise you, I will not be causing any trouble today. Could you call Russell? Please? Let him know Greg is here?"

Eyeing me up and down, the concierge, whose name is Michael according to his nametag, seems to consider this.

"Michael," I go on. "Please. If he says he doesn't want to see me, I'll show myself the door. I promise." My chest constricts at the thought of such an outcome, but it's a very realistic outcome. Russell might simply refuse to let me up. Then I'll be forced to leave and figure out another way to get close to him.

Warily, Michael lifts the phone to his ear, his eyes locked on me the entire time. "Mr. Mailey," he says into it after a few seconds. "Mr. *Greg* is here to see you." A pause. "Yes, sir, *that* Mr. Greg." He goes quiet again. "Yes," he repeats, glaring at me with even more intensity than he already was. Again, a few beats of silence. Then, very unenthusiastically, he says, "Very well," and hangs up.

I hold my breath, waiting for him to speak.

"Mr. Mailey says you may go up."

I exhale. "Thank you," I say and start for the elevators.

The whole way up, my mind is in chaos. Alone, in the claustrophobic space of the elevator, I'm suddenly aware of how loud and uneven my breathing has become. A part of me wants to turn around. That's the part that's ashamed, scared. The part that understands that what I'm about to do will be done out of pure desperation.

But I have no other choice. This is the only realistic solution I can think of. The only chance I have of keeping my beloved Cristian.

In front of Russell's door, I close my eyes and take a couple of deep breaths, just like I did earlier today with Kate at lunch. When I reopen them, I'm still trembling with nerves, but I'm pretty sure this is as calm as I'm going to get.

I lift my hand and rap my knuckles on the door.

As I wait, I think about the first time I laid eyes on Cristian in that crowded bar in Madrid. About the way his thick eyebrows twitch with concentration whenever his entire world becomes the painting he's working on. In my mind, I see him waiting for me on our sofa, smiling from behind his big, pre-bedtime glasses. I remember that all he has to do is hold me and whatever I'm upset about at the time just melts away.

The hallway is silent. I can hear blood whishing through my

own ears.

I imagine myself waking up at home, months from now. Getting up to find Cristian cradling our daughter in his arms. Kissing her tiny, delicate head, and then Cristian's faithful lips. I envision being in the room when she stands up for the first time and says her first words. I imagine celebrating these precious moments with Cristian through laughter, through touch, through tenderness.

The door opens.

Russell Mailey stands before me. He's still in his work clothes, although he's pulled out his shirt from his pants. On his face is a calculated, condescending smirk. The one I've seen so many times before. Like millions of tiny bubbles, my hatred for him resurfaces. I can't lose my Cristian to this man. I won't.

He doesn't say anything. As if utterly unimpressed by my visit, he just turns his back to me and starts walking towards the kitchen. What a fool, I think. I could lunge for him right now. He wouldn't even know what hit him.

I don't say anything either. I step inside his posh, movie-poster adorned apartment and pull the door closed behind me. Holding my breath—my throat dry, my heart hammering—I wait for him to turn around.

Before he does, however, I hear his voice.

"To what do I owe this surprise visit?" he asks, the words booming through the vast space, even though he doesn't sound in the least surprised. On the contrary, it feels like he'd been expecting me all along.

When I don't respond, finally, he turns around.

And when he does and looks me straight in the eyes, waiting for me to answer, a surge of tears obscures my vision and a powerful sob swells within me. Shutting down all my defenses, putting all of my vulnerability on display, I fall to my knees. And as I set that sob free, the words I've been holding down come rushing out with it.

"Please," I say as tears stream down my cheeks. "Please don't take my Cristian."

Chapter 34

Triumph. That's what I'm convinced I see flash across Russell's face before his expression eases into something like pity. Again, he keeps me waiting, taking his time to reply. For a moment—which feels like forever—he simply watches me continue to degrade myself with my knees on his beautiful hardwood floor, my tired face streaked with tears, and my body trembling with desperation.

"I'll do anything," I choke up.

Russell crosses his arms but stays silent.

"I don't know what I can offer you," I keep going, "but there must be something. Whatever it is, I'll do everything in my power to provide it. I promise. Just, *please*, give me this one thing."

Russell studies me for another moment before he stirs. Slowly, he takes a step toward me. Then another. My heart is pounding in my throat but I stay put where I am, still kneeling on the floor. I'm still shedding tears, too, but now that I've made my plea, my guard is quickly rising back up.

The whole time, as he approaches, his arms still crossed,

his gaze is locked with mine. I hold it, my chest rising and falling. Russell's entire apartment is silent save for the sound of my
shallow, rapid breaths. The closer he gets, the more I sweat.

When he's only a foot or so away, his crotch hovering in
front of my face, he stops. His eyelids lower. Quietly, he purrs
the word: "Anything?"

Looking up, I swallow and give him a firm nod.

Russell's arms uncross, but his hands don't fall to his
sides. Instead, they push away the hanging hems of his shirt and
find their way to the front of his belt. Gently, he tugs the leather
strap out of its loop, releases the prong and slips the strap out
of the buckle until both ends of the belt are dangling. Next, his
fingers pop open the button of his pants and lower the zipper,
deliberately, all the way down.

This is so unexpected, so unlike all the other possible
outcomes I've envisioned, all I can do is freeze up and watch.
How is this even possible? Russell despises me. Doesn't he? Or
is this some kind of power thing? With the belt and zipper both
open, his black briefs peek out of his pants. He reaches for my
chin and pushes it upwards. "Are you really sorry?" he asks in a
strangely delicate tone.

I nod, my chin finding resistance from his fingers. He's so
close, I can smell his citrusy deodorant. The scent is familiar.
Intimate. Despite myself, despite hating this man more than I've
ever hated anyone, I'm already well on my way to an erection.

He smiles in an almost *kind* sort of way. His fingers slide
from my chin to my mouth, where his thumb, in a tender manner, pries open my lips. Again in that gentle, almost caring tone,
he says, "Show me how sorry you are."

And with that, with his other hand, he pulls down the front

of his briefs and releases his completely hard cock.

Surreal doesn't even begin to describe it. I never thought I'd do as much as speak to Russell again, not to mention set foot in his fancy apartment.

But this?

Our grunts and flared nostrils. The little slaps and scratches. All the aggression and distaste I feel towards the guy adds another dimension to the pleasure. It enriches it, makes it more potent. This time, our power play doesn't feel like a performance.

As a result—and I can't fucking believe I'm actually saying this—the sex is incredible. It's incredible when Russell maneuvers me around until I'm down on all fours on the floor, and it's incredible when the roles reverse and I have Russell bent over the kitchen counter. It remains incredible when he's on his back on his sofa with my fingers firm around his throat, and when he has my face pinned to his King-sized bed, his grip pressing down on the back of my neck.

Afterward, we lie side-by-side in silence, panting at the ceiling of his bedroom. The sharp smells of our cum and sweat and deodorants permeate the air around us. In this moment, I have no idea what Russell's thinking, but I'm afraid of breaking this strange spell. I have no idea what it all means, either, but I'm hoping it's a step closer to getting me what I want. Hopefully, it's a form of closure. An end of one era and the beginning of another. A new one where Russell is no longer a part of my life. One where he leaves me and Cristian alone. If, right now, I say the wrong thing, I risk veering him in the opposite direction. So, I wait for him to speak first.

Eventually, he does.

"I really liked you, Greg," he says. I suck in a breath and hold it. "I *really* fucking liked you. I had such high hopes for us. You were my first kiss."

A familiar anger swells within me. But I grit my teeth and keep quiet.

"That kiss happened for a reason," he goes on. "I spent the better part of my life wondering what you were like, who you turned out to be. Just wondering." He chuckles under his breath. "Until I decided to stop wondering and actually find out."

My entire body stiffens.

"The truth is," he says with a sigh, "I've been following you for quite some time, Greg."

A gush of unease blasts through me. "What?" I croak.

"Not so much while you were in Spain," he reveals. "But when you moved back to the States, closer to where you come from, closer to *me*, I took it as a sign. Unfortunately, although I wanted to, I couldn't reconnect with you right away. I was in a relationship, you see, for years, and, as you know, I honor my commitments."

My breaths have grown shallower but I do my best not to show it. So I was right. Russell had been obsessed with me for years. All this time, the gut feeling telling me that there was more malice, more *depth* to his actions than he was letting on, was correct. I shouldn't be surprised, but the revelation takes me aback.

And it makes me angrier.

"So you always knew my relationship with Cristian was genuine," I say, as non-accusingly as I can muster, which isn't easy. "And that we were open."

Another sigh from Russell. "I did," he admits. "That's what

I assumed, yes. But I didn't think of it as reason enough *not* to take my shot. After all, you'd never met me as an adult. I had to give you that chance. How could you possibly know that Cristian was the one for you without ever getting to know the person *I* turned out to be?"

On the bed, at my sides, I squeeze my hands into fists.

"So, when things didn't work out with the guy I was committed to, I finally made my move and found you on Tinder. You didn't admit to me that you were married, but I actually took that as another good omen. I thought, huh, maybe he's looking for a way out. I wanted—I hoped—to *be* that way out for you." He pauses. When he speaks again, his tone is much more bitter. "But you couldn't see our potential. You treated me like any other one of your sluts from Grindr. And then you dismissed me like that, after I *gave* myself to you. I felt so battered, so...*angry*."

I'm losing my patience, fast. My own anger is growing hotter, choppier. Still, needing him to tell me everything, I say, "I know." I try to sound encouraging. I've already demeaned myself. As long as it gets me what I want, I can take this. I can bear it to the end. "I deserved to be punished," I add for good measure.

"Right away," Russell goes on, "I asked Elijah to make contact with you. The kid would do anything I asked in exchange for a bigger role in my next project."

I grunt in acknowledgement but don't say anything. Oddly enough, hearing this part about Elijah pleases me. I prefer the idea of Elijah doing what he did to me to advance his career over the idea of him actually being in love with Russell.

"The original plan," he continues, "was for you to grow to

like Elijah enough so you'd be upset when he dumped you for me. He was supposed to dump you, obviously. Not the other way around. Anyway, I wanted you to see my value, realize that other men—men *you* desired—desired me. I wanted you to regret what you did to me."

"I do, by the way," I say, faking sincerity to the best of my ability. "I do regret it." The air-conditioning in the room has cooled my sweat and tightened my skin, but I don't move, fearing that if I do, I'll stop him from revealing more.

"Still," he goes on, "I kept thinking about the way I handled our encounters. And I wanted to give you another chance to redeem yourself—without any outside forces, like Elijah. And so I called you. Remember? And what did you do? You not only blew me off again, you told me about how you were closing up your marriage as soon as your baby was born." He snorts. "That part, I definitely did *not* know about."

I try to maintain my breathing under control. More and more the presence of Russell's body beside mine—so close our elbows and feet touch—repulses me. Still, I say, "Again, Russell, I'm sorry."

"That's when I knew I couldn't just rely on Elijah," he goes on. "My gut was telling me to do more. To give you another, *bigger*, push."

My pulse accelerates. "A bigger push?"

"Yes," he says. "To help you see clearly."

I go still, but my mind is swirling. What the fuck is he talking about? He went after Cristian to help me *see clearly*? Not to punish me?

"I like Cristian," he says, matter-of-factly. "I really do. And I get that he means a lot to you. You've been with him for eleven years. It's admirable. To be honest, me dating him and seeing how much it hurt you, only showed me that you can be a loving, devoted person, Greg. I always believed that about you."

"Thanks," I mumble.

"But," he says, "you're confused."

"Hmm?"

"You coming over today and begging me on your knees like that? It's wrong."

I swallow. "How so?"

"Cristian isn't the one for you. *I* am."

With a snort, I pull myself up into a sitting position. "What?"

"Surely, you understand now." Russell props himself up on his elbow. There's a disturbing fervor in his blue eyes. "After what we just did? After how we *connected*? Don't tell me you didn't feel anything."

"I didn't," I say, firmly. "Russell, the sex was great, but that's where it ends."

Russell sits up all the way. His eyes are even crazier than they were seconds ago. "Don't you see?" he says. "Cristian is an obstacle to our happiness. I know it's scary but you have to let him go. You have to take that leap."

I laugh. I can't help it. "There is no *our* happiness."

"There is."

"*No*, there *isn't*." I let out a huff of disbelief. "So, this whole time, you were trying to break Cristian and me up? So *you* could be with me?"

"You can't see straight because of him. We need him out of the picture."

Again, I laugh because this man is utterly insane. "You're out of your mind."

This, obviously, is not what Russell wants to hear. His nose wrinkles. Through clenched teeth, he says, "He's not good enough for you."

"Russell, stop," I warn. I'm no longer laughing. Shit-talking me is one thing. Putting Cristian down is another.

"He's a nice guy but he's holding you back in so many ways. You shouldn't be with a failed artist."

I breathe faster. "*Stop*," I repeat. The way Russell's dismissing and insulting Cristian—*my* Cristian, who clearly cares for him—like he's nothing, like he's a nuisance who never meant anything to him, makes me want to strangle him.

"Greg, be honest with yourself," Russell hisses. "Cristian's a *loser*."

That's what does it. My hand flies through the air and attaches to his throat. "Shut the fuck up!" I bark, pressing him back down to the bed and immediately climbing on top of him. But Russell's strong and he's angry now too, and he's already reciprocating. Before I can pin him down, he manages to kick me off.

Now that we're both on our feet, facing off, scowling, one daring the other to make a move, the smarter thing for me to do would be to stop, calm down, before things escalate. Before I do something I regret.

But the arrogance in Russell's features, the entitlement, the absolute assurance that, in the end, he'll get what he wants pushes me over the edge.

Like a naked quarterback, I lunge into him, shoving him into the wall with a giant thud before tackling him to the floor.

I'm straddling him, the bulk of his body thrashing beneath mine. Sharp stings of pain radiate from where his punches land on my ribs, my liver. The fucker is quick and strong. My head snaps back sharply when he jabs me in the face.

"Get the fuck off me," he demands.

Again, I manage to clasp his throat. All ten of his fingers rush over to dig beneath mine but my grip on his neck is tight. In this moment, I'm perfectly willing to end him. He's a bad person. The world would be a better place without him.

Before I can commit to the idea, though, his fist arches through the air and pummels the side of my head. Disoriented by the flash of white, throbbing pain, I loosen my grip on his throat. Jostling me off, Russell manages to slide himself away. As soon as I'm back up on my feet, he smashes into me, sending us flying—me first—into a tall lamp that goes crashing to the floor.

This time, Russell's the one on top and it's *his* hand around *my* throat. "We're meant to be together," he's saying. "The sooner you accept it, the better."

With everything I've got, I topple Russell off me. In a flash, we're on our feet again, our sweaty bodies clashing, wrestling, heaving back and forth, propelling each other first into one wall and then another.

It must be the noise we create. Next thing I know, there are new hands—ones that belong neither to me nor to Russell—around my wrists, and there are new, *clothed* arms around my naked chest, pulling me away, separating us.

Startled, I thrash around, enough to get out of their grip and see that they belong to two men I've never seen before. But there's a third person, in the doorway, too, who I do recognize. It's Michael, the concierge from downstairs. A powerful urge to scream pushes against the base of my stomach. Here and now, I hate these men from keeping me away from Russell as much as I hate Russell himself.

"The police are on their way, Mr. Mailey," Michael's saying, his voice firm over my grunts of resistance. "We'll take care of him until they get here."

I whip my face back towards Russell, who's standing there, naked, gasping for air. There's a bleeding cut on his lip and a giant sneer on his face. But he doesn't give Michael a reply. He doesn't even acknowledge him. Instead, he looks me straight in the eyes and says, "You can't fight fate, Greg. We're connected." He cracks his most sinister grin yet. "You're stuck with me for good."

CHAPTER 35

The sympathetic policewoman doing my processing at Precinct 1 in Tribeca allows me to make a phone call. As I don't have it memorized, she looks up Cristian's number in my contacts and reads it out loud to me as I dial.

"Thank you," I say. She gives me a weak smile and steps back.

I'm bruised, shaken up, and pissed off. But I'm also pumped. My plan might've gone completely off the rails, but my visit to Russell's apartment wasn't in vain. At least I now know, without any doubt or exaggeration, that the guy's an obsessive psychopath. And it was such a huge relief to discover that his feelings for Cristian aren't genuine. That Cristian was just a pawn in his sick game to get to me.

After Michael, the concierge, and his men broke up the fight and removed me—as naked as they'd found me—from Russell's apartment, they kept me in a locked utility room until the police got there. I tried to explain to the officers what happened, but, at the end of the day, I was the intruder getting violent inside Russell's home.

"Greg?" Cristian says as soon as he answers the phone. "Where *are* you?" There's alarm in his voice, but also love and worry, and I'm so happy and relieved to hear it, my temper deflates, leaving a growing shame in its wake.

"Mi amor," I say, my voice weak. "I got arrested."

"Puta madre. You *what*?"

I'm suddenly slapped awake to the fact that, although *I've* learned the truth about Russell, on Cristian's end, nothing has changed. Which means he might, once again, think I'm acting like a paranoid lunatic. And which also means he still cares about him. Loves him. The thought that Cristian was slipping away from me—could *still* be slipping away from me—is almost too much to bear. "I went to see Russell."

"Huh?" he exclaims. "What the *fuck* for?"

"We got into a fight. He admitted to stalking me for years and—"

"Are you out of your mind?" Cristian interrupts, his voice rising in both speed and volume. "What were you thinking? Coño!"

"I'm sorry...but listen to me, he doesn't love you, he was only—"

In a torrent of Spanish—mostly Spanish curse words—my husband continues to convey his disappointment. The longer he talks the guiltier and stupider I feel. Nearby, the policewoman shoots me a quizzical look. "I couldn't let him steal you away from me," I plead, trying to get some words in. "I couldn't lose you, so I—"

"What the *hell* are you talking about?" he snaps.

I gulp. This is the moment of truth. I can't deny or avoid it any longer. My voice shrinks. "I know how you really feel about him."

"Tell me," he demands. "*How* do I really feel about him?"

Through the knot in my throat, I say, "I followed you. I saw how you are with him. And I saw the painting, Cristian…I saw how you see him…"

For a couple of beats, Cristian is quiet. "What painting?"

"Don't act like you don't know. The painting in your studio."

Another beat of silence. Then: "Are you *fucking* serious?" he yells so loud his voice sounds static-like through the phone. "*That's* why you went to fight him?"

"How could I not? I had to fight for you. For us. I didn't intend for it to get literal…But listen, mi amor, he's a really sick man. He's—"

"Do you know *why* I painted that painting?"

I go quiet. My grip on the handset tightens. "You've never painted me," I whisper.

"He commissioned it!"

"Stop," I say, firmly. The idea that Cristian can bring himself to straight up lie to me like this right now is almost as painful as the actual thing he's lying about. "We both know you never accept commissions."

Cristian's voice softens. "Well," he says, "guess what? This time, I did. He was paying me ten thousand dollars, Greg. *Ten thousand.* I didn't want to paint him but I wanted the money. For us, you *idiot.*"

A heavy feeling of dread presses into my chest. "No," I say. "That's not true. You wouldn't have hidden that from me if it were true."

"I fucking had to hide it from you!" Cristian yells. "With how you were acting? You even said you never wanted to hear about him again."

My voice is stuck in my throat.

"I wanted to surprise you with the money. I wanted to contribute, Greg, because I know that sometimes I can be a burden."

I squeeze my eyes shut, but a tear manages to push through anyway.

"You always worry about money and you work really hard," Cristian goes on, little hitches tripping his words. "I wanted to help. So when he said he'd pay me that much money for a portrait of him—"

"But I saw you two in Harlem," I interject. "I saw how intimate you were."

"That was our last dinner together!" Cristian sputters. "After that, I was only going to see him at his office to deliver the painting."

This shuts me up. But not for long. Because there's one more thing. One *major* thing. "But you want to stay open," I say. "You want to keep seeing him."

"Dios mío, that's not why," Cristian sounds tired. Like he's running out of fuel. "My relationship with Russell has *nothing* to do with it. I talked to a therapist. A professional. She told me that closing up the marriage *and* a new baby at the same time could be too much. I *told* you this. Ever since we decided to close, you seemed so stressed out about everything. Your anxiety was acting up. The whole thing was putting too much of a strain on you." He releases a drained sigh. "Russell and I are done."

Those last words leave me speechless. But slowly, their meaning begins to take shape. And then, within me, relief swells into a huge bubble and bursts out in a stream of tears. This time, they're happy ones.

Cristian has managed to explain everything. Eliminated every doubt and suspicion I might've had. Every doubt and suspicion, I now realize as a sense of guilt and shame builds within me, I never should've had in first place.

As if reading my mind, Cristian says, "Mi amor, *why* didn't you talk to me? Hm? *Why* didn't you trust me? Trust in *us*? I always trusted you. Monogamous or not, I held up my end of the deal. I never doubted your love for me. Not once. Isn't that what our relationship is all about? Isn't that what we agreed on?"

All at once, I feel so stupid and ashamed and unworthy of this wonderful man's love. "I'm so sorry, mi amor. I was such an idiot." I'm about tell him how much I love him, how much I fucked up and how I'll make everything up to him, when I hear a shuffling sound on his end. "Mi amor?" I ask in a panic. "You there?"

"Hold on," Cristian says and puts me on hold. I wait, my heart banging.

One minute passes. Then two.

A crackle. I stiffen. "Hello?" I say. "Mi amor? Everything okay?"

"I have to go," Cristian replies. "Amelia's in labor."

CHAPTER 36

I'm only at the precinct for another hour. My pleas to be let out because my daughter's in the process of being born probably help, but it's a phone call from Russell—or his lawyer or someone else he's got wrapped around his finger—that seals it.

Allegedly, he's not pressing charges. I'm neither grateful nor impressed. If anything, I loathe him even more for putting me in a position where I could miss my child's arrival in the first place. Truthfully, though, the more minutes that pass, the less I think about him. Now that I know Cristian and I are going to be okay, he's not a threat anymore. These past few months, he's sucked up enough of my energy. Today, on this momentous day, I refuse to let him remain significant.

The taxi ride from the police station in Tribeca to the hospital in the Upper East Side takes another thirty minutes. In the car, I call Cristian, but he doesn't pick up. I start to freak out, imagining the baby coming into the world without me, but a few minutes later, he sends me a text. Amelia's contractions are growing more frequent but there's no baby yet. I exhale with relief and will the driver to go faster.

At the hospital, the staff is already expecting me. I give them my driver's license and a nice, bespectacled lady leads me to Amelia's birthing room.

Inside it, on the bed, I find my squirming surrogate in a hospital gown, a nurse looming over her on one side and Cristian kneeling beside her on the other. He's holding her hand. As soon as he sees me, he kisses it and whispers something in Amelia's ear. Too fixated on her agony and breathing, she doesn't even react.

Cristian runs straight into my arms. I'm so weakened with relief to feel his familiar form, to smell his reassuring scent, I explode into a shudder of happy tears. "You're here, mi amor," he says into my neck.

We kiss, long and hard, and Cristian brings me up to date on what I've missed, which—thank God—didn't include the main event. As he talks, I become mesmerized by Amelia. It's like she's a sun—full of fire and energy—and everyone else in the room is a boring, rocky planet orbiting it. Her face is redder and shinier than I've ever seen it before, and her hair clings to her forehead in wet clumps. She looks mighty, transcendent. I feel a warm surge of respect and gratitude toward her.

"You've got this," I call, hoping to throw her some encouragement.

Her eyes snap up, latching onto mine. "Shut the fuck up, *Greg*," she growls.

I raise my palms up, defensively, but there's a small smile on my lips. In that moment, I decide to leave all the supportive talk to Cristian.

When Amelia's contractions stabilize and she seems to have her breathing under control, one of the nurses, as there are now two, says, "This would be a good time to grab a snack or a coffee." She winks at me. "It'll be a while still."

Cristian and I trade a look and nod in agreement. He sneaks over to the bed to let Amelia know we're stepping out. He asks her if she needs anything but she shakes her head and dismisses him with a ruthless, "No."

In a quiet daze, my husband and I make our way over to the lounge. There, Cristian pulls out the sandwiches he ordered on the way from Brooklyn. I realize I haven't eaten anything since my lunch with Kate. I'm starving.

Ripping into the food, our coffees steaming from paper cups, we stare at each other, smiling, basking in each other's presence. I absorb the familiar landscape of Cristian's face. The thick eyebrows and the thickening scruff, the light wrinkles around his eyes. I know it sounds cheesy as fuck, but looking at him like this, knowing that he still loves me and that we'll soon get to meet our first daughter, together, really does make me feel like the luckiest man on earth.

But then Cristian's smile dims and his gaze falls to his sandwich.

"So," he says. "You got arrested on the day of our daughter's birth."

My stomach sinks. I wish that part of my day—and everything that preceded it—could be ignored and forgotten. Even a tiny dip back into my memories to the excruciating sense of loss and despair I felt just hours ago is enough to cause my chest to constrict and my armpits to sweat. Talking about Russell and the police station will surely taint this once-in-a-lifetime experience that my husband and I are living through at this very moment. But I've made my bed. I have to lie in it.

Cristian's eyes meet mine. He waits for me to speak. Ashamed, I falter, wondering where to begin, how much to tell him now and how much to leave out for later. I guess my inner predicament must be written all over my face because his expression lightens and, shaking his head, he says, "You know what? I don't even want to know."

There's a flutter of relief in my gut. "Really?"

He lowers his chin and asks, "You're never going to see him again?"

Resolutely, I nod. "*Never.*"

"Good," he says. "Then let's leave him behind. Let's never talk about him again. For real this time." He smiles.

My smile is more hesitant. "But…you still have that painting to deliver."

Cristian shakes his head. "No."

"No, what?"

"I'm not going to do it."

"Didn't he already pay you for it?"

"Yeah, but I'll refund him the money."

I swallow. "What about the painting itself?"

A smirk weaves onto his lips. "You can help me destroy it."

I laugh. "Deal." Cristian is laughing too and I rocket out of my chair to give him a kiss, getting a whiff of Swiss cheese on his breath in the process.

When I sit back down, though, I feel the thorn of dread I've been trying to ignore ever since I left Russell's apartment. Because the truth is, I'm not sure I'll ever be able to leave the guy behind completely. Cristian doesn't know, but Russell's obsession with me runs deep. *Deep* deep. Finding out that he'd been tracking me for all these years unnerved me to the core. If he's done it in the past, what's stopping him from doing it again in the future? As long as that man is alive, will I ever feel truly at peace?

"Natalia," Cristian says, jerking me out of my dark thoughts. There's a timid, loving look on his face that instantly banishes Russell from my mind.

"I always liked that one," I say. "You grandma's name."

"My all-time favorite, I think."

I beam at him. "It's perfect."

Natalia comes into this world a little over three hours later. First, I see the blood-speckled surface of her tiny head, then her tiny shoulders and arms. Our shirts already off, ready for skin-to-skin contact, Cristian and I watch her unveiling, not wanting to miss a single second. But we can't help glancing at each other from time to time through tears in our eyes, our laughter drowned out by the sounds of Amelia's toil.

When Natalia's out, Cristian cuddles her first, but I'm right there beside him. Whenever I'm not taking a million pictures, I'm gently pinching her miniature fists and pudgy thighs. "She's so beautiful," I declare, predictably, about a dozen times. But that's the word that best encompasses what I'm seeing and feeling.

By the time Natalia makes it into my arms—her tiny, delicate form warm against my naked chest, my husband at my side—I'm full on bawling. So much happened in the months leading up to her birth, so much darkness. But we managed to survive it, we pulled through. Russell Mailey might've left me battled and bruised—both literally and figuratively—but I'm still standing and I'm stronger than ever.

In the grand scheme of things, Russell is, always was, nothing. He's crazy, sure, but my anxiety and paranoia made him out to be a bigger threat than he actually was. Because, at the end of the day, there's nothing he can do to penetrate the love Cristian and I share. There's nothing he can do to disrupt it. Kate was right. It's what Cristian and I—and now Natalia, too—have that's untouchable.

Later, in a private postpartum room, Cristian is cradling a newly weighed and cleaned-up Natalia in his arms. Amelia's in bed, exhausted but glowing as she watches him with a thoughtful expression. I wonder what she's thinking. I feel a pang of sympathy and sorrow for the woman. But it's okay, I remind myself. She knew what she was getting into. And, if she chooses, she can be a big part of Natalia's life.

Taking a break from snapping a million more photos, I step up to Cristian and move aside the soft little blanket Natalia's wrapped in so I can see her face. Her big eyes are unfocused, but for a brief second, I could swear they meet mine. A surge of happiness dampens my vision. "Did you see that?" I ask Cristian. "She looked at me!"

Cristian smiles, intuitively, but his eyes—permanently fixed on Natalia—betray the fact that he's lost deep in thought. There's a furrow between his brows and his jaw is set tight. And even though he just smiled, his expression is unmistakably solemn.

My blood freezes in my veins. Again, I look down at my daughter.

Up until this point, I didn't give the icy blue color of Natalia's irises much thought, even if both Cristian's and Amelia's are brown. Lots of babies are born with eyes that later change color. Everybody knows this. There was no reason for concern.

But Natalia will always have clear, blue eyes, won't she? They won't be changing, will they?

About the Author

Sebastian J. Plata was born in Poland, grew up in Chicago, and spent most of his twenties in Tokyo. In addition to writing,he also works in the subtitle translation industry. He is currently based in Brooklyn, NY. Seeing Strangers is his first thriller. Find him online @sebastianjplata.

ACKNOWLEDGMENTS

Lori Galvin. The best support system, kick-in-the-ass provider, and, of course, literary agent a guy can ask for. This book is what it is today because of your input, enthusiasm, and perseverance. Thank you! Thank you! Thank you!

Chantelle Osman. Thank you for taking a chance on this story and for all the hard work you put into polishing it and putting it out there.

Family and friends—love y'all. Special shout-out to Amelia. I might use your name in the book or something, not sure yet.

And, finally, a big thank you to all the dudes I've met in the past and have yet to meet in the future who inspired the dudes in these pages. You're all great. (Well, most of you are, anyway.) Stay safe out there!